ZANE PRESENTS

NO MORE TOMORROWS

TWO LIVES, TWO STORIES, ONE LOVE

Dear Reader:

No More Tomorrows is hands-down, one of the most touching novels that I have ever read. Then again, that should not come as a surprise, in that Rodney Lofton's memoir, *The Day I Stopped Being Pretty*, also struck a major chord with my emotions. Rodney's ability to flesh out the characters in *No More Tomorrows* comes naturally. Unlike those of us who can speculate about what it might feel like to be HIV-positive, and those of us who cannot begin to imagine dealing with the effects of the disease for decades, Rodney has done just that. Thus, in creating a love story between Mark and Kevin, Rodney has written one of the most beautiful romances; he has shown what unconditional love truly means and it resonates throughout the pages.

There were many points throughout this novel that I found myself crying. At other points, I found myself blushing; I felt like I was being given an intimate peek into someone else's flourishing relationship. There were even times that I was envious. Even though this book is about a homosexual couple, as a heterosexual female, I crave the same type of love that the main characters share. If only more people could embrace each other's differences, work through relationship issues, remain faithful, and take commitment as seriously as Mark and Kevin, the world would be a much better place.

I am very proud to present *No More Tomorrows*, a book that will serve to remind all of us that every day is truly a gift that must never be taken for granted. Some people believe that money and material things are the true measure of a man's life. The true measure of a man is his character, who he was loved by, who was loved by him, and the mark he leaves on the world. The true measure of a man's character is not what others see him do, but what he does and how he lives his life when no one is watching.

Please let me know your thoughts on this book. You can reach me on Planetzane.net, or email me on Eroticanoir.com

Blessings,

Zane

Zane
Publisher
Strebor Books International
www.simonandschuster.com/streborbooks

ZANE PRESENTS

NO MORE TOMORROWS

TWO LIVES, TWO STORIES, ONE LOVE

RODNEY LOFTON

SBI

STREBOR BOOKS

NEW YORK LONDON TORONTO SYDNEY

Strebor Books
P.O. Box 6505
Largo, MD 20792
http://www.streborbooks.com

ISBN 978-1-59309-174-5
LCCN 2009924322

First Strebor Books trade paperback edition June 2009

Cover design: www.mariondesigns.com
Cover photograph: © Keith Saunders/Marion Designs

10 9 8 7 6 5 4 3 2 1

Manufactured in the United States of America

For information regarding special discounts for bulk purchases, please contact Simon & Schuster Special Sales at 1-866-506-1949 or business@simonandschuster.com

The Simon & Schuster Speakers Bureau can bring authors to your live event. For more information or to book an event, contact the Simon & Schuster Speakers Bureau at 1-866-248-3049 or visit our website at www.simonspeakers.com.

To "Ian"
Thank you for closing the doors to my fears
and opening my eyes to life.
I am no longer afraid.

"Through all of my life
Summer, Winter, Spring, and Fall of my life
All I ever will recall of my life
Is all of my life with you."

—Alan Bergman and Marilyn Bergman

ACKNOWLEDGMENTS

The great Stevie Wonder once said,

"Much has been written about
The world and all its kind of loves
But the sweetest of them all
You seldom will find stories of"

As a black man, many great stories have been written about the love he feels and shares for his woman, the one that sets his soul on fire. Songs have even been created to symbolize his passion for her.

As a gay man, many books and films have covered the genre to show the "taboo" love, hidden in the darkest of nights, behind back doors and unspoken for fear of being cast aside or ostracized.

As an HIV-positive man, rarely do you read stories of loving in the face of adversity. The trials and struggles of those living with a disease that cuts short one's life.

Here I attempted to incorporate for this often forgotten community, of which I am a part of, to show we live and we love.

Believe me, it was certainly no easy task. After my debut offering, *The Day I Stopped Being Pretty: A Memoir,* I found it very difficult to share with you, the reader, a story, which is both foreign and elusive to me, a story of love. I found myself frightened by the prospects of letting you down and not meeting or exceeding your expectations with my follow-up. Many wanted to read a "what happened to…" continuation to *The Day I Stopped Being Pretty*, but in time, that will come. I wanted to stretch myself and delve into something that I only dreamed of in my life, a loving relationship.

On numerous occasions, I found myself starting and stopping because I didn't know where to begin. Fear consumed me as I thought of you and not wanting to let you down. But I lost sight of why I wanted to write; I wanted to write for me. And that's what I did.

I found two people who came into my life and allowed me to share with you their story. But before I get to them, I need to thank others.

God, I can't believe You have brought me so far in such a short time. You know my heart for I was made in Your creation. You smile with me; You cry with me. You have shown me love beyond compare. You guide me and You forgive me and because of that, I am much wiser and stronger. Thank You.

To my mother. You are truly the wind beneath my wings. You offer love when it is so needed and you offer guidance when I lose my way. I couldn't have selected a better mother/friend if I had chosen you myself. Thank you for choosing me.

To my family. Thank you so much for your continued love and support. I know at times it is difficult to love me as I am, but through it all, you are always there.

To Zane and Charmaine Parker. I cannot begin to thank you both for this wonderful second opportunity. The road was rough after the release of *"Pretty"* but the two of you stuck by me and weathered the storms. The two of you offered me more than a publishing deal, you extended love and friendship. I will be forever grateful.

To my Strebor Family (both past and present): Tina Brooks McKinney. What can I say to you that I haven't said to you over and over again? I love you! You have laughed with me, cried with me and even cut-up with me. You never sugar-coated anything for me and I so appreciate you for that. Like Helen Baylor, I had a praying grandmother and she sent me an angel on earth in the form of Marsha Jenkins-Sanders. I always felt the hand of your spirit guiding me over the last two years, spreading the word of God. You will always hold a special place in my heart and you will always know why. Lee Hayes. My brotha by my otha motha, Jackie Washington. Man, I am so proud to call you my friend. I have enjoyed laughing with you and trading barbs. Don't forget our special day—Jackie Washington Day. Allison Hobbs. I have three words to describe you: FAB BOO LUST! You welcomed me into the family with open arms and showed me how to hustle. Thank you. Laurinda Brown. From the first conversation to our very last, you always inspire me. You have shared your wisdom with me, and I truly appreciate it.

Lissa Woodson. You and I will share a moment unlike any others I have shared. I will never forget you taking hold of my hand and allowing me to let go. I thank you so much for that. Shelley Halima. You are one bad sistah!!! I aspire to be half the writer you are. Always remember, I've got your back! To David Rivera and Che Parker: Thank you for embracing Rodney the man. I have learned from both of you and I take those lessons with me wherever I go. To the rest of the Strebor Family, thank you so much for your continued love and support.

My friendships are what keep me grounded. When my head becomes too big for the world, M'Bwende Anderson, Shaun Ferrell, Ronald Drake, Kevin Pollard, Tony Kemp and the crew at Barcode remind me where home is. Thank you. Each of you has touched my life and my heart in a special way you will never know. I love you all.

To the wonderful people I have met along the way over the last two years. Terri Williams, Ella Curry, The Sweet Soul Sistahs Book Club (especially you, Royce, and Jacki), my girl Tina in Atlanta, Ms. Anne from Norfolk, VA, RAW4ALL, Tee C. Royal, Tokes Osubu and the staff of Gay Men of African Descent and everyone who stopped by and offered a smile, a hug, a kind word; thank you.

To the brothers and sisters living with HIV/AIDS. Please know the struggle is not yours alone. My thoughts, prayers and love are with you. Remember to live life to the fullest. Love like it is going out of style. Live like it is your last day on earth and celebrate the joy of simply being.

Lastly, I need to thank two people who have come into my life. I don't think I know of other writers who have thanked characters from their writings, but I need to thank the two main characters of *No More Tomorrows*.

To Mark, thank you for allowing me the pleasure of writing and developing a character living with HIV with dignity. You provided a voice in this pandemic that speaks volumes of courage and conviction. Through it all, you lived in the moment, never once giving in or giving up. I now live to love like you, with passion and determination.

To Kevin. Thank you for being the man I have dreamed of the last fifteen years. You are one who embodies understanding and compassion. I hope readers will see you as I do; a man determined to love *because of* and not *despite of*.

I don't know what happens now. I don't know where the road of life will lead me. All I can say is how truly thankful I am for the journey. I am excited to see what is ahead on the road, around the bend and over the hill. I am open to the great possibilities of this world, because I am no longer afraid, to live, to love and to celebrate. I hope my writing has in some small way, shown you what it is to grow as a black man, love as a gay man and live as an HIV-positive man. As I said, I don't know where I am headed, but I thank you for keeping me company along the travel. It is my hope that we can continue to learn and grow from the trials and tribulations of our past. I have come to the realization that it is time to let go and let love. Thank you once again for your continued support and opening your heart and soul to reading about one of the sweetest love stories never told.

With love and appreciation,

Rodney Lofton

MARK

I awoke from the same bad dream that had haunted me for the last few weeks. The T-shirt stuck to my body from the drenching sweat during the tossing and turning in this horrible nightmare. I lay for a moment so not to disturb him. He slept peacefully as I fought the demons in the dream. I opened my eyes and replayed the scene as I stared at the ceiling.

It started out simple. I saw the image of me as a little boy, playing jump rope. The game of choice, "A Little Higher," allowed me to tell my little girlfriends to raise the height of the rope to showcase my ability to leap higher than the others playing the game. I laughed as I made my way to the front of the line. It was my turn to increase my chances of winning the game. Then I heard it: "You ain't nothing but a sissy."

Fast forward to high school. After fighting with my father numerous times for the designer jeans my fellow classmates adorned, I was relegated to the neatly pressed dress slacks and oxford shirts he selected for me. His son would follow in his footsteps of best dressed. My feet longed for the days of the past summer vacation, where I had walked the streets barefoot. But now I was confined by argyle socks and dock siders. I maneuvered my way through the halls, greeting classmates and teachers. My smile had gained me recognition among my peers. Between classes, I stopped at my assigned locker to retrieve my books for the next set of classes. My hand missed the slamming of the door from the jocks as they parted the hallways with their broad shoulders and letterman jackets, leaving behind their stinging phrase: "Punk."

The next stop on this lurid journey, I saw myself exiting the Red Line's 1 train in New York's the Village. History had shown me this was the one place where I could be myself without judgment and fear. I ascended the stairs, searching the faces of beautiful men passing me. I smiled, acknowledging the looks I received, hoping in return that the Southern charm I was accustomed to would be returned. I only received, "You fucking faggot." Each time, like clockwork, I would awake at the same step, facing the same menacing look that shattered the disturbing night of attempted slumber.

I had to change my T-shirt since there was a chill in the air. I managed to pull myself up and swing my legs to the side of the bed. As my hands rested and I braced myself to stand up, I felt the dampness of the sheets from my side of the bed. Damn, not again. I didn't want to wake him yet again to change the sheets. This time I would allow him to sleep. I found my footing from the aching neuropathy, reaching for the cane that had become my constant companion as of late. It felt like I was walking on a bed of nails as I hobbled to the bathroom closet. I needed to retrieve an extra sheet to cover the damp spot where I would return shortly. I made my way into the bathroom, searching for the light switch with my available hand. As the fluorescent light brightened the small cramped bathroom, I caught a glimpse of me. I stared at the man in front of me. I didn't recognize him. I had known him all of my life and now he was a complete stranger. His face was gaunt and pale. His cheeks were sunken, never providing any indication of the roundness they once possessed. The sparkle in his eyes was now replaced with deep, dark circles. The smile that captured the hearts of many now reflected the parched, dry, cracked lips, which ached with the simplest touch. Who was he? I searched his face, searching for the answers. I realized, much like the dream, that man was *me*.

I couldn't cry anymore about my circumstances; they were what they were. I looked deeper into the vacant eyes staring back at me, searching for a brief glimpse of the man once called "pretty." The man who had charmed those with his well-disguised insecurities. I searched the lines that ran the length of his face, as each one told a story of love found and lost. Along those lines, were moments of laughter, moments of tears. Those were the days.

I decided to ditch the idea of a new T-shirt and removed the terrycloth robe hanging on the back of the door. If I continued down this horrible memory lane, I would find somewhere a reserve pool of tears, but I didn't want to tap into them. I ran the tap long enough to cup a handful of warmth to bring to my face. Ahh, it felt good. I patted my face dry and made my way back to our room.

The sun peeked through the shades, interrupting any thoughts of returning to bed. I eased my way into the recliner he had placed next to the window for moments like this. There were times I found it difficult to sit for long periods in the living room and make the walk down the long corridor to our bedroom. He wanted me to be comfortable. I rested my head on the back of the recliner and watched him.

His back was toward me. The sunlight showcased his beautiful brown skin. The outline of his back stood out prominently. My eyes traced the nape of his neck, down to the top of his boxer briefs, accenting the curves of his ass. I was lucky to have found him. He was clueless of my absence as he continued to sleep. I simply watched him; taking in every mark of his body, the few strands of hair on his back, the neatly shaved bald head. This was my mental photograph to treasure, for I realized it would be one of the last images I would have of him.

KEVIN

I lay there quietly. I heard him stirring about as he attempted to silence his movements, being careful not to disturb me. As much as I wanted to reach out to him, he hated that. He was fiercely independent and although he knew I did not mind, I didn't want to take away this last bit of independence from him. I knew what happened when I felt the moisture from his side of the bed. It was that damn dream. I wished I could have taken it away from him, like so many other things I wanted to protect him from, but I couldn't. I could only allow him to be. I fought with myself to get up when he did; I felt a void when he wasn't beside me. I followed him as he walked into the bathroom, knowing all along this was something I could have taken care of. I wanted him to rest, but he wouldn't have it. When I saw the lights go dark in the bathroom, I closed my eyes, continuing to play the role of Sleeping Beauty, oblivious to his movement. But what I didn't see, I felt with each step—each painful step he made to that old recliner he had grown to love. It was the only gift that I could give him to make this easy.

My throat tightened, wanting to say something, but honoring his pride prevented me. I felt his eyes embrace me and I returned the embrace with my thoughts. We had talked about this moment so many times. What would we do? What would we say? I could hear him call out to me in his heart as I reached for him with mine. The time had come for us to say good-bye.

MY SIDE: MARK

I t was hard to believe that twenty years had passed since I entered the doors of the old building. I stood there watching others enter and exit as I did twenty years ago today. It was as if time had stood still. The building had not changed, maybe a power wash or two to clean it up, but nothing else. The grounds of the property remained the same, littered with the debris of street trash from the gusting wind, settling to find a home from the savage cold. I watched the faces of the men and women as they came out of the big doors, searching for clues to see if their smiles, or their tears, would reveal their futures. Like poker players, they carefully kept their cards and their answers to themselves. I watched as they wrapped scarves around their faces—not to protect them from the cold, but to hide the unfortunate information they had received. Part of me wanted to offer a kind word of support, a hand to hold, but I remembered the day for me as if was yesterday and the empty feeling I felt when I received the news.

My eyes began to water as I thought back to that day, the one that changed my life. Hearing the phrase: "You have tested HIV antibody positive." I shuddered as the thoughts ran through my head again. Back then, there weren't a lot of advances in medicine or treatment for persons living with HIV. I was told by so many that I would die and I believed it. I spent the greater part of the last twenty years preparing to die, only to awake one morning and realize it was a diagnosis, something that I would have to contend with for the remainder of my days.

The flashbacks of my life played out in mere moments, but the thoughts were so vivid and detailed; I relived them in my dreams. I made a promise to myself back then if I made it to twenty years of living with HIV, I would return to the place where life changed for me and prove that HIV was not a death sentence. As I stood there braving myself to enter this place, I was saddened by what I saw.

I pushed the heavy doors, making my way into the building. I relaxed my jacket a bit as I looked around. The faces that adorned the posters had changed from the days when I had first visited. No longer hanging on posters were photos of emaciated white gay men. No, the faces had changed to showcase beautiful brown-skinned women, holding delicately the lives of their children in their arms. The young faces of the Chelsea crowd of New York were now replaced by butter pecan-flavored Latinos from Washington Heights. The faces and ages had changed, but the outcome was still the same—HIV POSITIVE. I noticed the brochures. They were now multilingual to address communities that had not seen the devastation I had lived with— losing friends and lovers alike to this horrible disease. At any given moment, I could take off my coat and replace the black and brown faces on the posters. The white face that greeted me with kindness years ago was substituted with a sister girl and her neatly cornrowed braids, adorning her head majestically. Her smile offered warmth to those seeking the answers to why they came here. She politely nodded in my direction, acknowledging my presence. Rather than tell her I had journeyed here on some sick anniversary, I picked through the bowl of condoms placed on her desk and returned the smile. I needed to get out of this place. I began to suffocate from the history I had created here and needed to make a quick exit. As I headed toward the door, the hallway seemed to elongate, making my exit longer and never-ending.

I gasped for air as the bitter cold slapped me back to reality. The doors closed quickly behind me, stifling the voices and the tears that I imagined would pour from the walls and the small offices. Each person would sigh of relief of dodging a bullet or hear those words that would do for them what they did for me—change the course of their life. I headed for the rental car and cried. I turned the music up so no one passing by could hear my sobs, not for me, but for many whose lives would change. Twenty years had passed and folks were still testing positive. I managed to pull myself together as I made my way to the tunnel to the Jersey Turnpike, heading back to my reality. I was alive. I had made good on the promise to live with this disease and to return to where it had started. The second part of the promise awaited me as I found my way back home to Washington, D.C. to celebrate this anniversary of living.

My friends thought it was twisted of me to celebrate twenty years of living with HIV. It was like a second birthday celebration. I had friends who actually turned back the clocks and shed years off of their actual lives, to remain young forever, even if the indication of their age showed by way of frown lines, age spots and the like. But not me; I was happy to see another year. I gladly wore my HIV status as a way of saying, "I'm still here." After I accepted that I was going to live, each year I treated myself to a cake with the correct number of candles to indicate the number of years I was living with HIV. It was wonderful to see a new candle burning brightly each year on the sheet cake that read, "Happy Living." This year was no different. I went about planning the same as I did every year.

Three weeks before the celebration of life, I finalized the details of my "Happy Living" party. The invitations were already in the mail and the RSVP's were coming in via voicemails and e-mail invites. Before I had headed to New York, I had solicited the help of friends to decorate the small, quaint house I was paying way too much for on D.C.'s Capitol Hill. I would have very little time decorating after returning from New York and wanted that out of the way.

xxx

The bar was stocked; the drinks would be flowing, along with the forced laughter for such an occasion. The German chocolate cake from Ben's Chili Bowl was placed as the centerpiece of the table, with the candles waiting to be lit. I counted them off as I placed each one around the celebratory phrase, "one, two, three," continuing until I hit the big 2-0. My friends were making a fuss in the kitchen, as I made my way into the shower to prepare for the party.

The hot shower felt good as it washed away the pain and tears from the quick visit to New York. I ran my hands across my body, caressing it, embracing myself. I held myself tight, hugging me as only I could. I was happy to be alive and knowing that I was alive made me cry. My tears of joy were lost within the water trickling from the showerhead. Hey, what can I say, I am a punk. I cry a lot. I stepped out the shower and took a moment to admire my body as I dried off. There was a little more of me to love, but it was distributed in all the right places. As I turned around to take in all of me, I carefully searched to make sure there were no visible signs of disease. Although it was a celebration of life, I still had the fear of finding something that wasn't there before I got in the shower. This would indicate to me that I was dying. I couldn't see it, but it was there. I quickly dismissed the thought as I continued to prep for the evening. I could hear the partiers from downstairs as I got dressed, checking myself in the mirror. Like Bette Davis in *All About Eve*, I wanted to make a grand entrance, but in a very butch way. Well, thinking about it, Bette was kind of butch in that movie. I smiled at the thought and descended the stairs. One of my friends was able to secure a couple of Cedric's mixed CD's for the party. I made sure to invite my neighbors to the celebration, to disarm them from calling the cops. Everybody likes free food and booze, even if they have to be subjected to throngs of men embracing, holding hands, sometimes kissing. Booze will make you look the other way—maybe encourage one or two of the closeted neighbors to take a walk on the wild side.

As I continued downstairs, I was a vision in black. The black Johnny Cash came to mind as I maneuvered the spiral staircase. The partygoers were given a revised version of "Happy Birthday" to sing, incorporating the phrase "Happy Living." My friends and family who came out to share this event with me were aware of it, but dates, new boyfriends of some, were unaware, but they went along with it.

I smiled as I saw my mom's face. She had weathered this storm with me. It was her hug and her love had gotten me through the most difficult parts of the last twenty years. Her arms were the first I reached for as I made my way off the final step.

I whispered in her ear, "You were right; we got through this."

I could feel the trembling in her voice as she responded, "I love you."

I didn't want to break down as I had done in the past. I allowed the embrace to linger for a moment and as we parted, I saw the happiness in my mom's round face. I listened as the words of the revamped song raised the roof of the house.

I made my way through the crowd gathered to celebrate with exchanging hugs and polite conversation. My friends had really outdone themselves on the budget that I had provided them for this occasion. Cedric's voice drifted from the speakers, inviting everyone to dance. Of course, there were those who stood around with their disapproving stares and thoughts, but fuck them. This was *my* party. I stopped at the makeshift bar and asked my buddy Sam for a shot of tequila and a Corona. The Cuervo burned a bit, but I was used to it; no training wheels here. I took a quick swig of the beer, soothing the burn, and made my way to the dance floor to shake what little ass I had.

I drifted in and out; eyes closed reliving the last twenty years. The days of hitting Tracks and the Bachelor's Mill came into play. I found myself on their dance floor with beautiful bodies surrounding me, sweat dripping off the finely chiseled and worked-out torsos that brothers had worked all winter to achieve. As I lost myself in these memories, I could see the faces of so many disappear from that dance floor. Those I had admired for their swagger, and had envied because of their six-packs, had vanished before my eyes in my dreams. Some I had the pleasure of entertaining on a more intimate and personal level faded away with each year I recounted. The crowded dance floor became empty as I searched for familiar faces and eyes to respond to, only to see empty spaces where they once occupied. This is what HIV did to our community—my community. I was left standing alone on the dance floor. The friends—gone. The lovers—gone. I stood there in my dreams, in my solitude, aching for someone to reach out to me, to see them once again, but it didn't happen. The music blared as I found myself spinning around, hoping to have others replace them, but no one showed. I wanted out of this trip down memory lane. I opened my eyes quickly to see the light. It was not time yet. It was not my time to head toward the light. The lights that searched for me were the burning candles of the cake.

My thoughts were interrupted as my hand was grabbed and guided toward the food table. There before my eyes were the candles reminding me of life. Unbeknownst to my well-wishers, was the heaviness my hard carried at this moment. The dream of the last dance with friends and lovers struck a chord with me. I longed for those days of carefree living and loving, but my reality was now constant doctor visits and a strict drug treatment. I managed a smile to disguise the sick I felt in my stomach. Each candle represented a year of life for me, but added more to the list of those who died. I heard the chorus refrain in my ears as I was encouraged to blow out the candles and make a wish. Blowing out the candles meant erasing their memories. I couldn't do that. My hesitation allowed the candle wax to drip onto the coconut. With the refrain, I heard the voices of those who went before me, celebrating this moment with me as well. They reminded me that I was still here and to take advantage of living. I would not be snuffing out their lives, but honoring them by living mine. I took a deep breath, inhaling the various scents, and held that breath. The chants of "make a wish" forced me to close my eyes and silently whisper my wish to myself. I was a selfish bitch; I wanted more than one wish, but I wasn't going to be greedy. I settled for two; the first wish was another year to live, to celebrate life. The other wish was always out of reach after being diagnosed: I wished for someone to love and for someone to love me. I blew out the candles, making sure to get each one with this one breath. As I opened my eyes, his eyes met mine.

❤❤

Love is a motherfucker. Like Stephanie Mills, I needed and sought the comfort of a man, but only found little boys pretending to be men. With a big smile, a trick hip became game and dishonesty. Many assumed I was desperate because I was living with a chronic disease. They figured my life expectancy was short, and I would put up with anything in order to have someone in my bed, or arms, for that matter. Initially, I found myself seeking out the love and attention of others. I needed to feel like the man I once was before being diagnosed with HIV. I wanted to feel desirable, so I found myself accepting anything and everything offered to me. There were the brothers who promised to be there through thick and thin, to wipe tears and offer comfort. But after they got their nut, they left. Then, there were the white boys, who became motherly and smothering. They were well-informed about HIV disease and the effects it had on the body and the psyche. But their concern for my welfare far out-shadowed any possibilities of simple love, patience and understanding.

So rather than focus on the love that would nurture me from someone else, I focused that search on myself. On that new journey, I discovered the true essence of me. In a moment of self-reflection, I found the greatest love that I could possibly receive was from me. The numerous faces and body parts that graced my door and bedroom were substitutions for what was truly missing—me. After this epiphany, I got my ass off of the couch and away from the number of sex websites searching for a temporary fix; I decided on some long-term goals.

For starters, I started to seek others who were like me. I found myself attending local support groups in the area, not for dating purposes, but for that uplifting support. I found it therapeutic to meet others like me, some long-term non-progressors, as well as some who were in the final stages of the journey. It was refreshing to share and hear from others what struggles we all shared—love, compassion, being ostracized and being embraced. I would walk away from the meetings at night, reinvigorated, energized and empowered. Sometimes it was difficult to attend a meeting and see an empty seat of someone you had come to love and respect because they were called home. It was moments like this that made living with this disease unbearable. But I would take with me the contribution that man or woman had made to my life. I held onto the thoughts, the words and the love they offered, without asking for anything in return. It continued to nourish during those moments of silent tears in the privacy of my own home to mourn their passing.

The next step was to work on the physical. I had spent the greater part of my life relying on the good looks everyone complimented me on. I was always able to maintain what God granted me, but I never took the time to work it out like talking about. That first day in the gym was intimidating. For a moment, I thought I was at the bar, watching these cock-diesel guys flaunting and strutting about the locker rooms like proud peacocks spreading their feathers. A couple of times, I caught my eyes drifting from head to toe of these men, noticing who was wearing a jock strap, and the one or two who allowed their manhoods to swing freely. I avoided the machines these men used; the last thing I needed was the scent of a smelly-ass crotch tempting me as I worked out. It was trying, to say the least. The taunts and looks of come-hither eyes, bodies I dreamed of, lying next to me. Damn. But I hung in there. I purchased an iPod and let my thoughts drift into the music and relax the burning muscles that ached from years of not working out. After a while, I noticed the difference. My clothes started to sag a little, but the ass I so hoped for was now developing. My gut no longer hung slightly over the belt that held it in place, and the definition of my chest started to show through my shirts. I took pride in discovering what was underneath the layers of life and fat in my new form.

The third step in this new path of life came in the form of career. I had spent my life working jobs, with no clear career path. I would stay long enough in a position until I grew tired of it, or it outgrew me. I was graced with life and a strong support system to help me carry the load of living with HIV. Therefore, I wanted to give back to the brothers and sisters who didn't have the support from their families and friends.

I found myself an old man among recent high school graduates maneuvering through the classes of Howard University to finish my degree in social work. Eventually, after graduating, I found a position at a national HIV/AIDS advocacy organization focusing on advocacy. I now had a career that allowed me the opportunity to address the concerns of persons living with HIV/AIDS and their allies. I was afforded the opportunity to travel and share the messages of living positive. At times, I found myself burning out from sharing so much of my story, depleting my spirit and soul. But it was so rewarding when someone was able to hear the message and make positive changes within their own life. I gained a little recognition doing the work. I was interviewed by BET and national newspapers for quotes and stats on HIV/AIDS in the African-American community. I almost felt like a celebrity. I would sometimes find myself in an airport making my way home from a conference or event, only to see the eyes of some checking me out. At times, I believed it was because of the new look and fresh outlook that drew these individuals to me. I could see the pensive stares as they attempted to remember where they had seen me. Some would be so bold, especially the brothers who were drawn to the newly formed ass, to approach me with some lame-ass lines, from "you look familiar," to "I think I have seen you before." I would acknowledge their statements and remind them of a recent interview I had conducted on HIV. The lust that initially greeted me was replaced with a hesitant, "oh okay," and a quick retreat. This would be my existence; the fear of being with me because I was positive, but there was a greater cause down the road.

On the flip side of trepidation, were those who wanted to take care of me. Some of the guys I found myself involved with went out of their way to protect me from any and everything. A simple cut or bruise became a possible trip to the emergency for them. I got to the point where I didn't want someone hanging over my shoulder all the time to protect me; hell, I had a mother for that.

So I found myself patrolling the internet, chatting up brothers and white boys alike. At first it was America Online. For a while there, you could chat men up in the neighborhood for friendship or no-strings attached sex. With some, I was honest about my HIV status, especially after seeing the photos they had sent. I was horny, not desperate. After revealing my status, some would respond with the obligatory "I'm sorry to hear that, but I can't risk it," or I would be blocked. In some cases, it was a blessing; even on a bad day, I wouldn't fuck them. Others, who knew about HIV and knew how to protect themselves, would be willing based on the photos I had sent out. Sometimes the photos were not of me. I wouldn't send a face pic to save my life, but I was able to find a dick pic that resembled mine. That seemed to secure me a date for the evening.

With some, it was the need for company. A nice glass of wine and some good conversation outside of the friends I shared my innermost thoughts with. Although it would end after they left, it was nice to have a "date" for a few hours. It was an end to the means of being horny for simply that moment. They would leave satisfied, and I was content, but there was a certain emptiness that lingered into the late hours of the night.

I became bored of AOL and moved on to bigger and better websites to curb my appetite for comfort and friendship. As always, it played out like the rest of the sites. So, I stopped looking and invested my earnings into good ol' porn.

Just like the internet, porn satisfied the savage beast. For all too brief a moment, I was able to do what I needed to do, without the thoughts of being misled, rejected or scorned. I was able to release myself in the privacy of my bedroom, grab the towel in the nightstand, wipe off, and turn the lights off.

This newfound "reconnection" with myself was working. I looked good, I felt good, and I was doing well in life. But in the back of my mind, was the lingering thought of love.

Coming out at an early age allowed me the fortune, and sometimes misfortune, of falling in love. With some of my past lovers, I found the connection that you sometimes dream of. With others, it was just to occupy time and space. Nevertheless, I found myself jumping from one relationship to another. I wanted what I saw on television and in motion pictures; the perfect house, two cars, maybe a kid or two, the white picket fence, but I wanted it all with another man. Some promised the possibilities of fulfilling those dreams, while others tainted them. But I always held out for the hopes in the back of my mind that it could possibly happen. I was, after all, a dreamer.

Unfortunately, being dealt the ultimate blow of an HIV diagnosis quickly turned those dreams into unreachable limits. I even stayed in the relationship with the man who infected me, only for fear of being alone. Here I was a relatively young man, in the prime of my life, living out my dreams I dreamt at night, only to have it all taken away with one statement: "You have tested HIV antibody positive." The relationship I was involved with was shaky. And as soon as it was confirmed for him I was positive, he continued to show his ass and treat me far worse than he ever did. I realized it wasn't good for me to stay in that relationship; not emotionally or physically. So I took what was left of me from that situation and retreated into myself. Walking away was probably the most difficult thing I could do. At that moment, I presumed that I would never find anyone who could love or would appreciate what I brought to the table. I never wanted anyone to complete me, just complement what I was able to offer. So the depression hit.

After wallowing in my own piss for a period of time, I woke up from the depression and realized HIV was no longer a death sentence. The only thing that was killing me was me. From that moment, I vowed to live, and if love presented itself, so be it.

In twenty years, I became the man that I dreamed of loving. I became the romantic paramour of my own needs. I treated myself, because no one could do it better than me. I loved me the way I wanted to be loved. I pampered me the way I wanted to be pampered. I embraced me on cold nights, the way I wanted to be embraced. For the first time in my life, I found the love

I so desired and wanted within myself. Like Iyanla said, "Clean your house and prepare it for yourself before you invite anyone in to share it." Baby, the house was Spic and Span clean, and I was ready for him. I stopped looking for him because I was looking in all the wrong places. I searched the clubs, the internet, searching for HIM. Little did I know that when I stopped looking for him, he would find me.

IT'S MY TURN: KEVIN

Now let me tell you upfront, I am not your average gay man. First and foremost, I am a black man; it is obvious by the color of my skin—deep, dark coal. Some call me blue-black and I wear it like a badge of honor. Growing up, kids used to say hurtful things like, "I can't see you unless you keep your eyes open or you smile." My momma was always there to make sure to heal the wounds of the hurtful words. With each passing day of my youth, she encouraged me to embrace the smooth silkiness of my beautiful complexion. It would become one of the many traits that would draw others to me.

That, and a big dick she knew nothing about, but I am sure she had an idea since I was made in the mold and the spitting image of my daddy. I knew I was my daddy's son when I caught glimpse of him accidentally stepping out of the shower. He was a proud, dark-hued man who had taught me confidence, character and conviction. Despite the jabs kids threw my way, I walked proudly with my head held high and chest rising above all the bullshit.

In school, I noticed the guys taking peripheral peeks at my abnormally large dick in the showers after a sweaty gym-class session. I smiled as I took my manhood in my hand, soaping the appendage, making sure to cup it in my hands to showcase the thick vein through the soap lathering the shaft. I would catch them looking before they darted their eyes away. I would close my eyes and laugh to myself as I rinsed away the soap residue and walked out sans towel.

Now, I knew at an early age I was gay. There was no sexual abuse or molestation involved that swayed my decision. Now, don't get me wrong, I am not taking a crack at those who were; my attraction was something that was always there. The same looks that greeted me in the showers after gym class, I more than willingly returned. It was hot to see brothers freely swinging underneath the steam from the hot water, soap running from the nape of their necks, sliding down slowly to rest right at the crack of their asses. Sometimes I found myself getting hard, but this was not the place for it. I would linger in the showers at times, giving my eyes the feast they desired.

One day after class, I stayed a little later than usual. I had the early stages of a pulled muscle in my calf and treated it with additional heat from the steam. I found myself doubling over in pain as I bent down, reaching for my leg to massage it. I was lost in the pain as I noticed everyone leaving, with the exception of the one guy we all made fun of.

He wasn't the most masculine brother in the school. I must admit I fell in with the crowd of classmates to make fun of him when he was unable to excel in the class. But he was cute. He was shy in his demeanor and self-confident enough to ignore the taunts of those who called him out. He broke my concentration as he asked if I was okay.

I continued to massage my leg as I winced in pain. He moved closer to me, resting his hand on my shoulder. He assumed I didn't hear because he asked again about my condition. I raised my head slightly to see genuine concern on his face. He wiped the water from his eyes and continued to look at me. I stood up, backing away from him for fear of anyone walking in, but by this time, the locker room was empty. As quickly as I stood up, he replaced my position; kneeling and extending his hands to my sore calf. He began to massage in a gentle, circular motion. What I couldn't do to relieve the pain, his touch did. He grabbed the soap, and lathered his hands to create enough foam to massage deep into the tissue. I rested my back against the shower stall enjoying the touch.

His hands felt good against my skin. I closed my eyes as I enjoyed his continuing touch. I was drifting back to those stolen moments of hidden gay porn magazines tucked neatly in the back of my closet. Never once imagining that the images I jacked off to would actually come into play in my life. As I focused on the touch and the images I played in my head, my dick hardened a bit. I felt more heat than usual around the head as I opened my eyes and noticed my masseuse was gently flicking his tongue across the head of my dick. He looked up at me, seeking approval. I silently acknowledged both his handiwork and oral skills without begrudging him the taste he wanted.

I got harder as the hot saliva in his mouth replaced the water from the shower. From his ability to relax the back of his throat to accommodate me, I knew he had done this before. I looked down at him as our eyes met. I was amazed he was more than able to take me in his mouth. I watched as my dick disappeared in and out of his mouth, all without gagging. The hand he used to relieve the stress in my leg was now making its way up and down with the same amount of soap and precision performed on my leg. I didn't want to appear to be forceful, but I couldn't help it. I grabbed him by the back of his head, my back securely resting against the wall to brace myself. I forced my dick deeper into his mouth, trying to hit tonsils. This brother had skills. Without pushing me off, he continued to open his throat deeper, allowing me to explore the joys of the back of his throat. Before I knew it, and with my fear long gone, I continued to pump the back of his throat, until I shot my load deep in his mouth. When I finished, he raised his face way up to mine, allowing the water to enter his mouth and gargle a bit. After spitting out the combination of cum and water, he leaned in and kissed me. I brought him closer to enjoy not only his full lips, but the taste I left him with. This would be the first of many shower encounters throughout our high school years.

After him and high school, there were the occasional brothers throughout college. Some were there just to blow me. On rare occasions, I found myself breaking one or two in the ass, but I was searching for more. Not that sex was a bad thing; I wanted something with a little more substance. I saw the images of the white gay men and their lives of living and loving another man, and that was what I wanted. You know the images —the perfect house or condo, with the two-car garage, two-income household, and the families that embraced this love between two men. It was initially difficult for my parents to come to grips with me being gay. I guess I didn't fit the image of what they had in mind when they thought of gay caricatures. But after some difficult moments, and at times, harsh words, they learned I wasn't going to change.

After college, I dated a bit, but nothing too serious. There was one man I met and fell in love with, but the drama of his bullshit turned me, and my heart, off to any others. Every time I turned around, I questioned the sincerity of brothers. Was it my heart they wanted or my dick? I could respect one if he came correct and upfront, but the beating around the bush shit wasn't my cup of tea. So it was with much reluctance I accepted the invitation to this dude's "Celebration of Life" party. There I realized the games no longer applied. It was there I would find the love I searched for.

THE JOURNEY BEGINS: MARK

When I opened my eyes, I saw him. He was the King of my dreams. Tall, definitely dark, and more beautiful than any man had the right to be. For a brief moment, I allowed myself to entertain the thought of loving such a fine brother. But who would want to deal with someone like me: black, gay and diseased? The possibilities seemed endless, yet far reaching. I allowed the hopes and dreams of life with such a specimen to fly away, all the while concentrating on his face. His smile was not a full ear-to-ear grin, but one of surprise and wonder at this spectacle. I sensed he was a bit uneasy, but that was his cross to bear and not mine. Before I could continue to search his face and reassure him of the party's purpose, friends and family grabbed at me to hug and offer kisses of congratulations. They knew the importance of this day and that was the most significant. The volume of the music drowned out the well-wishers and partygoers, as everyone now focused their attention on themselves and the fine eye candy gathered for my party. Between the hugs and gushing, a shot of tequila was thrust into my hand to celebrate the moment. After downing two shots, I searched for a Corona to take the sting off. The shots traveled throughout my bloodstream as I closed my eyes, bopping my head to the bass heavy sounds. Arms from guests and exes found their way around my waist, with the occasional crotch brushing against my ass. The party would last until the wee hours of the morning, and I had to slow my roll if I was going to enjoy it. I was pulled onto the makeshift dance floor as others gathered around me. I cried silent tears of happiness and sadness as I thought of those who should have been here. Mannie, the beautiful Puerto Rican roommate with a Napoleon complex from Brooklyn, who showed me the ropes of living in the Big Apple, teaching me how to cook corn beef and rice and the joys of Salsa dancing; Adrian, the sexiest man I had ever known, who mothered me when I found out I was HIV-positive, offering the love and support that the one who infected me couldn't manage to give. There was Keith, wiping tears from broken hearts, offering love, with a stern hand and promises of better loves to come. Waving to me beyond the crowds was Peter, the man who fulfilled every fantasy I had of what a man could be—sensitive and caring, patient and understanding. Standing beside him was James, with bowlegs and all, showcasing the latest dance style that had won him a scholarship to the famed Alvin Ailey Dance Theater. Sprinkled in the crowds were the others, celebrating with me, loving me, holding me, and living within me.

I grabbed the third shot that was offered to me and celebrated with my friends and their memories. Each one continued to teach me about life and love, and escort me on this journey.

I was the center of attention and it felt good. Life was good. I held my face so no one could see the tears inside or the invisible mascara run. I wanted to do what I had set out to do—celebrate. All the while eyes waited to see me crack under the strain of this disease coursing through my veins, fighting for space alongside the tequila. But I wouldn't have that. And although I performed, there were a set of eyes that continued to see through the game.

KEVIN

When I heard about the party I'd grudgingly agreed to attend, I thought what kind of sick motherfucker would throw a party celebrating living with a disease. My boys tried to help me remember him, but for the life of me I couldn't. When they told me he was light-skinned and pretty, that described half the men living in Washington, D.C. Besides, I never really featured the high-yellow pretty boys in the District. They were some of the most vain, self-centered assholes I'd come across. Always stopping to check themselves in the mirror, talking to one brother while checking around to see who was watching them. They were the type to avoid sweating while having sex, for fear of messing up the permed and pressed hairdo that led them into club. I didn't need that. My plate was full enough with the day-to-day shit of work and being a Black gay man.

I was out and proud, not only in my personal life, but my professional life. So I didn't have to deal with the talking behind my back, or speculation of who I was fucking, or, on the very rare occasion, who was fucking me. Now, I wasn't a card-carrying member of HRC, the Lambda Legal Defense Fund or any other gay advocacy group, just a Black man who happened to love his brothers. I carried myself the way my momma and dad raised me, like a man. They taught me a man is defined by his character and how he treats others and not what he does in the privacy of his bedroom. As I said earlier, my dad had a difficult time with me coming out. In his day, he was used to the effeminate man doing hair and promenading like a woman. I loved visiting the two of them on Sundays for a home-cooked meal and spending the remainder of the afternoon catching a game on television with my dad. I sometimes caught him taking in my "gayness" as I yelled at the television, checking to see where my eyes were glued. He was right to think I was checking out the asses of the football players, wondering how much weight my shoulders could withstand from the thickness of their thighs and defined calf muscles. All the while I was swigging a beer and simply being a "man." I miss those days with him; we were the best of friends and he raised me well. When I visit Momma on Sundays now, I try to get her riled up when we watch a game. She's a good sport, but not like Dad.

Although there was some hesitation on my part to attend, there was nothing else going on that night. I could roll with my boys, get a couple of free drinks and a little grub, and head down to the Fireplace. Since Tracks and the Circle Bar had closed, the closest thing to a decent bar was the Fireplace; sometimes that was hit or miss. Oh, what the hell, that was D.C. for you.

When we arrived at the party, I saw some of the old familiar faces from the bar and other house parties, sprinkled in with some new ones. It was a little weird though. The party was tight; some decent-looking brothers, some I would probably fuck on any given night, but now I hesitated. With this party being a celebration for someone living with the bug, I assumed everyone around me was carrying it. There were one or two I had broken off a while back, and I thought about the times I had been with them. I had managed to miss the hit, since they were back in the day. My most recent test results had come back negative. I decided to make the best of it, get a few drinks, and break out. That's when I saw him. As he came down the steps, I recognized him immediately. Yes, the description was true to form and fit him to a tee. He was light-skinned and yes, he was pretty. He was most definitely not my type.

I recognized his face as I remembered each time I had seen him out. In between the smoke and the intense fog machines at the club, I would see him taking up space in the corner. He was like the other redbones I had dealt with in the city. Yes, he was pretty, but in a very masculine way. I had noticed him a couple of times out, unassuming and quiet. He wasn't raising the rafters, running from side to side with a tambourine to raise the already deafening noise of the club. Nor was he the type of brother I saw pretending to walk the runways of a fashion show, pivoting on his toes, mocking all those unnecessarily highly paid, stick-thin models. I would watch how others checked him out. He would smile politely and pleasantly, which indicated his momma had raised him right. He would sometimes hold court, brothers fawning over him, but I guess he was used to this. But there was one thing that stood out each time I saw him: He always left alone. Sometimes I would think about walking up next to him to have my dance card filled for the evening, but shrugged it off. Now, I knew why he never left with anyone; he was positive.

I guess I'm wrong like a lot of men. When you hear that phrase, your hard dick tends to go south. It makes you think back to all the times you let a warm mouth or a hot ass back up on you raw. That was a hell of a reality check. I guess those brothers who had thought they could hit decided it was not in their best judgment to go there with him. But what struck me about him, if he never told anyone he was positive, no one would ever know. He had a tight little body on him and a very suitable ass. He didn't look like someone who was sick or dying. I remember seeing the movie *Philadelphia* with Tom Hanks and seeing lesions covering his body when he was testifying on the stand. I didn't see anything on this brother's naturally chiseled face. So I wondered, why tell anyone if they are going to reject you?

I became engrossed in my thoughts as I focused my attention on him. I had dealt with some guys who wouldn't tell you they were poz until you were about to enter the spot. So this told me a lot about this brother's character. I watched him as he thanked everyone who had come out to share in this morbid celebration.

His smile and hugs were greeted with kisses and handshakes. I wasn't stupid about how the disease was spread, but I wouldn't willingly kiss a brother who was positive on the lips for fear of catching something else. Call it what you will; that's not ignorance, it's a precaution.

I continued to watch him, in between brothers and the handful of white boys trying to slip me their number. If I didn't know what I knew, I would easily forego the skin complexion thing and that pretty face. Damn, why are all the decent-looking men fucked?

I heard the music cut off as everyone made their way around the well-lit cake. I wanted to take another look at him before I finished my drink and bounced. I bogarted my way to face him. His head was bowed as he silently closed his eyes and made his wish. All but one candle was blown out as he raised his eyes. With the remaining flicker, I saw what so many others had failed to see from where I was standing: I saw beauty, I saw fear, but the most important thing I saw was love.

MARK

The excitement of the party was taking its toll on me as I tried to tap into a reserve of energy to see the rest of the evening through. I didn't want to be a spoil-sport, but with the drive back from New York, and the course of the evening, a brother was tired. As the evening grew, there were those who came and said their good-byes as they headed out or hooked up. But through it all, I kept my eyes on the brother who caught my attention when I blew out the candles. I watched him standing in the corner taking everything in. I sensed that he was somewhat uncomfortable and I didn't want that. I wanted everyone to have a good time. Each time I made my way closer to him to check on him, someone would distract me and take my attention away. Every now and then, I would notice that he would change his location, making it sometimes difficult to spot him. Over the years, I had lost the nerve to approach guys when I knew I had to reveal my status at some point. This was different, however. By this time, he had to have known, but rejection was still a hard pill to swallow. I saw friends of mine checking him out, and holding conversation with him, so I dared not interfere. I continued to hang out and watch the crowd thin out with each passing hour.

I decided to take a seat and rest my weary body and feet. I took this moment also to try and catch up with the liquor I had drunk. I closed my eyes and rested my head against the back of the sofa, trying not to fall asleep, and listened to the muffled voices through the music. I almost drifted for a moment when I felt a hand grace my thigh. I quickly opened my eyes and saw my best friend. Standing next to him was my vision of beauty. I looked up at him as he towered me, looking away to see who was watching us. My buddy encouraged me to stand as he introduced us. I couldn't hear his voice as I traced his full lips with my eyes. Oh, to kiss those lips. I leaned in to ask again his name.

His lips brushed against my ear as he whispered, "I'm Kevin."

I felt a hot flash coming over me as I savored that all but too brief touch. I could only stutter, "Thank you for coming," as I leaned in again, wanting to feel his lips against mine.

KEVIN

I caught a whiff of his scent when I leaned into him. I had smelled the patchouli knock-offs before, sold at the street corner stands, but here it left a mark on me. His boy was trying to play matchmaker for me, but I was a little gun shy. There was something intriguing about this brother, but I couldn't get past the HIV thing. I simply couldn't. Maybe a different time and a different place, maybe, but not now. I remembered vividly the first time that I was confronted with the disease. In very similar circumstances, I had met a brother at a party that I started to kick it with. He was a well-put together, brown-skinned brother, with an ass you could set a dinner table on. Like this brother, Mark, he possessed those same set of eyes that would capture your attention and make you focus and hold on to his every word. I attempted to make my way through the crowds of brothers sniffing after him to at least take a chance at getting to know him. I had been turned down by brothers in the District before. I wasn't one of the pretty redbones they all sought. I was cocky enough to push aside the others to get his attention. What I liked about him was his candor and his honesty. He wasn't one of those shallow motherfuckers into superficial shit—you know, the job title, latest cars, or neighborhood association. He was just a brother looking for love as we all had searched for.

It was early on in the epidemic, when brothers who used to

dance their weekly frustrations out on the floors of the Clubhouse every Saturday night didn't heed the messages of some
new disease targeting the gay community. In between the heavy
bass lines and tabs of acid we all dropped on occasion to free
our inner souls, we didn't hear what was happening in the gay
population. Well, actually, we heard it, but we didn't listen. At
the time, the images that we saw of gay men dying from this
new disease that attacked the immune system were white gay
men. There were no images of us. And I suspected the brothers
who spent the fall and winter months working on their bodies
to showcase on the Clubhouse dance floor—sweating profusely
and gyrating to the beats and round asses all around—certainly
weren't checking for the white boys of Dupont Circle. But we
were not immune to it. The brothers who proudly walked the
floors, showcasing the latest dances, bodies built by months
and years of conditioning and gym time, started to evaporate in
front of our eyes. The grace, with which they commanded the
attention of all partygoers, became awkward shells supporting
bodies that had taken a beating from something, or some act,
that would take their lives. The brother that I mentioned became
an unwilling victim of those days of unbridled drug use and
anonymous sex partners.

I noticed, as we got to spend time and get to know each other
better, before attempting to tap that ass of his, he started to
disappear in front of my eyes. I never suspected anything outside of a cold or the flu, depending on the season and time of
year, but he continued to get worse. I even jokingly asked if
maybe he had caught the "gay cancer," as it was called back in
the day, after walking through the lily-white gayborhood of
Dupont. He swore on his mother's grave that he had never been
with a white man in his life. If anyone had cause to be alarmed,

it would have been me. White boys traced the outline of my dick with their eyes each time I walked along the streets to make it to my final destination. I was nothing more than a big dick, a fantasy. The big Mandingo buck, there only to satisfy the whims and pleasures of ol' massa. But what we didn't know, or what we elected to ignore, was that the "gay cancer" was silently killing the brothers in our community. The dance partners we searched out to turn it out on the dance floor started to disappear. Then the government told us how it was spread in a public service announcement. Regardless of whether you slept with a white gay man or not, who were the initial victims, they told us it was spread through bodily fluids. We didn't know much, but we knew the acid that drove our desires to reach the mountains through dancing, produced large amounts of perspiration. Thus, it was the beginning of the end. Eventually they, the government, mind you, would later come out with the truth of how the disease was spread. But there was a panic in our community. We saw DJ's that spun the hottest tunes, the buffed bodybuilders we all lusted after, and the occasional queen we would fuck without telling anyone, vanish. The dance floors were now empty and brothers were dying.

He eventually became one who disappeared. One minute he was there with me, laughing over dinner, chilling at his place or mine, and the next minute he was dead. A casualty to the most innocent behavior we all searched for in the Clubhouse, Tracks and the other bars we sought refuge in: love. Over the years, I counted my blessings numerous times that I had been fortunate enough to avoid contracting the plague. I knew too many guys who had died. And the way the disease disfigured once good-looking model types was unforgiving. Boney and pale, looking like death walking, I only imagined what would be done to this

brother standing before me. As he released my hand, the soft-
ness of his small hands began to work on me. I was fighting a
sudden battle within that came upon me suddenly. Here, standing before me, was everything I wanted and everything I fought
long and hard to avoid. In that brief moment, he reminded me
of the first guy ever to really play with my heart. I played out life
with him. In quick succession, we would date, fall in love, make
love, then he would get sick and die on me. I couldn't put myself
through that, especially after seeing what the first brother went
through. So, I said my thank-yous and good-byes, and I forced
my way through the crowd and out the door. I stood there on the
porch, facing the door, contemplating returning to the party, but
I decided against it. I turned away to head toward my car, and I
noticed his face once again peering out the window. I saw the
disappointment through the slight smile on his face. I was yet
another man, who would turn his back on him; it was because
of what he had instead of the man he was. Damn, I didn't want
to rain on this man's happiness. It took a lot of balls to do what
he did tonight, a celebration of life. And here I had taken the joy
away from him because of my own private fear and fucked-up
insecurities and stereotypes. As I turned the key to start my car,
I decided I needed to make it up to this brother.

MARK

The one thing I hate about parties is the cleanup. I stood there looking at the task ahead of me. Queens are famous for eating and drinking up your shit, but they get lost when it's time to clean up. I had a slight headache from the tequila the night before. I needed to address it before I tackled this mess I was left with. I grabbed a couple of Tylenols and some water and sat down until they kicked in. I was deciding what I needed to focus on first; the spilled drinks and dropped food, or the decorations. When I felt the relief of the Tylenols kick in, I pulled out my Nancy Wilson collection. I was not in the mood for any bumpity-bump bass lines this morning. I opted for the silky voice of Nancy on a much toned-down volume. Nancy always had a way of soothing me. Through good times and bad times, she was that good girlfriend who celebrated with you with songs like "Grass is Greener" or betrayal of a loved one with "Guess Who I Saw Today." I allowed my bare feet to sidestep the mess on the floor, picking up shit that was tossed in a corner, with hopes I wouldn't discover how trifling mother-fuckers were. I ignored the rings of the house phone, allowing the callers to go into voicemail. These were the "girls" who wanted to continue partying because they knew I still had liquor and food left over. Not today. Today would be the day I cleaned house, took a nice hot bath and relaxed. Besides, I felt bad.

Not from all of the excitement, but from being irresponsible. I had decided against taking my medications because of the party and I knew I would be drinking. I was pretty good at not missing doses for fear of building up resistance to them. But, this one night of all nights was special. On top of that, mixing Sustiva and tequila tends to fuck you up. It's bad enough that Sustiva causes depression at times and affects the central nervous system. I didn't want to compound the feelings of loss with alcohol. I would have been a suicidal bitch, in more ways than one. In order to claim the reward of a hot eucalyptus bath followed by a stretch across my bed, I needed to finish cleaning. Nancy raised her voice to me; she guided me through the next few hours.

I looked around the room and I had to admit I was proud of myself. If I hadn't been here the night before, I would have never known there had been a party. I could still smell the scent of the Pine Sol I used to mop the kitchen floor and the air freshener that cut the odor of cigarettes and reefer. I have to admit, I did allow some folks to puff a joint while here, but not in front of everybody. I threw on some sweats and tennis shoes to take the trash out to the bins. Upon returning to the house, I realized the temperature had dropped outside from the previous day. This was going to be a great afternoon of resting. I made my way upstairs, checking to make sure the bathroom was cleaned. There were a few folks who had missed the toilet from pissing the night before, but luckily, there was no vomit to clean up. I took a moment to freshen up my sanctuary before I ran the bath.

I retreated to my bedroom and picked out a pair of pajamas. I rarely wore things that confined me at night outside of a wife beater. I loved going commando. There was something very satisfying about lying in bed naked, but today, I just wanted to pamper myself. I returned to the bathroom to check the water and added a few drops of eucalyptus to soothe me. It would take a few minutes for the water to cool down, from the steam rising. While I waited for this to happen, I returned to my bedroom and changed the sheets. I wasn't about to sleep on the sheets after the party. God only knows who had crept up here to get a quick blow job or a quick hump, leaving a little of themselves on my bed.

After the bed was made, I returned to the bath. I ran my hands gently across the water to test its temperature. I would have to brave the heat because my body longed for release. I quickly undressed and began to submerge myself. I stood there bracing against the shower bar and caught a glimpse of myself in the mirror. I took myself in as I stood there naked. I ran my hands across my body, enjoying the touch. It had been a while since anyone, let alone me, had touched me. My mind shifted from the scalding water as I continued to look at myself.

What was wrong with me? As I examined, I saw a man with a somewhat nice body. I saw my face that showed no true signs of age or destruction. I turned around to admire myself from behind as others have in the past. Facing the mirror once again, I continued to wonder what was wrong with me. It had been twenty years and there were no visible or telltale signs of the disease, yet it continued to repel potential lovers. I was a catch to some, until those words were uttered, "I'm positive."

I was going down a road I couldn't allow myself to travel. These moments of self-woe and self-pity hit me at times like a ton of bricks. But this time, I couldn't do it. Only the night before, I was celebrating being alive with others. Here, I stood wanting to cry for being alone, for being positive.

I decided against letting this get to me. I submerged myself in the tub, enjoying the fragrance of the oil now wafting through the air.

After what seemed like an eternity and the water had cooled down, I re-emerged from the tub feeling like a new man. I moisturized my skin and placed on the pajamas. I retreated to the kitchen for something quick to eat and drink before I returned to my bedroom. I turned the television on, flipping through the channels to find something to doze off to. I crawled underneath the covers, feeling relaxed and drained. I turned the volume down to a low hum as I thought about the party. It had turned out better than I had expected. I was still a mix of emotions, but in hindsight, I had enjoyed myself. I pulled the covers up to my chin to warm me from the chill in the air. As I closed my eyes, I thought of him once again—Kevin. I touched my ear where his lips had brushed it, when he whispered in my ear over the noise. With my eyes closed, I saw him standing there in all his chocolate beauty. I allowed the thoughts of him to rock me to sleep in this beautiful dream, even if it was a dream never to come true.

KEVIN

I lay there with my hand resting on my nuts, my eyes fixated on the ceiling. When I got home, I jumped out of my clothes and left them in a pile at the foot of the bed. It was easy to fall asleep after a long day at work and going to old boy's party. Looking up, I couldn't help but think of him. For the life of me, I didn't know why I couldn't get him out of my thoughts. I saw his smile greet me as I turned over to look out the window, undeterred by the noises coming from the street. I continued to shift uncomfortably, thinking about him. *Why?* I thought. *Why is this brother positive? Why did he let someone run up in him raw? What the fuck was he thinking?* I kept asking myself mental questions I didn't know the answers to. Each time I convinced myself it wasn't my issue, I found myself returning to his face. His smile lit up the room, all the while knowing he, at some point, was going to die. He had a tight, little frame I could mold and shape into positions of brothers I had fucked in the past. The thought of that made my dick hard a little. But the one thing that continued to remind me of him were his eyes. I had gone to bed thinking of them, and now I found myself lying in bed thinking of them. They were trusting eyes. The eyes we want to see when we come home from a long day at the nine-to-five. The eyes that will tell you when he is happy and the eyes that will let you know you have hurt him. All without saying one word. Those are the eyes that have me lying here totally fucked up.

When I left the party, I saw those eyes say good-bye to me as they have said good-bye to many others. I wanted those eyes to say so much more to me.

I finally got my ass out of bed and made a cup of coffee. I turned the television to find out the latest on the news as I thought things out. I wasn't a dumb man, by no means. I was just a scared man. From the images back in the day, it was easy to tell if someone had the "curse." You could tell by the abnormal weight loss; with some you could tell by the marks on their skin. Or at least that is what I told myself. Over the years, I saw brothers on the verge of death, but with the advances in medicine, they were brought back to life. Some even took this as a second chance at life, pumping up their bodies by hitting the gym, re-creating themselves in the face of death. Those signs of death had disappeared, and there, standing before me in the clubs and bars, were new men, with old diseases. I avoided them, I have to say. No amount of muscle would make me venture their way after seeing them at their very worst. I would see a change in their appearance, but their behaviors continued. I watched some leave with different men night after night. The medications and the gym only prolonged the inevitable, but did not create a change in their attitudes toward fucking. What a sad rollercoaster to be on. *If only HIV had changed the mental as well as the physical, how much better they would be,* I thought.

Call me judgmental; I will admit I am. I had avoided infection a couple of times. I must admit I wasn't always safe, but the fear of infection made me overly cautious. I assumed I could wash it off after pulling out and seeing that a condom had broken, or I let some brother suck my dick. That fear can kick you in the ass when you face the reality of possible death. I would throw my dick in the sink at any time given the circumstances. I can't begin to tell you the fear someone feels when they are sitting in that waiting room, having someone ask you a million-and-one questions about your sexual history before they stick that needle in your arm to draw blood. I knew for certain I wasn't one hundred percent honest about what I'd done and who I'd done it with. I would sometimes lie about what I'd done, fearing that I had put myself out there one too many times.

After they draw your blood, you spend the next two weeks or so praying to a God that you are negative. Sometimes you find yourself making promises you know you will never keep. Promising the next time, if the test comes back negative, you will use a condom each time, even when you get your dick sucked. But as soon as you get those test results giving you the go-ahead, what do you do? You run to the first hot mouth or piece of ass to blow your load. And the cycle continues. The promises and negotiations with your God fly out the window when your eyes are closed and you enjoy the moisture coating your dick.

That probably had happened to him. Each time he went to the doctor for the test, he made promises. He promised that he wouldn't allow anyone to fuck him raw. But he did. He promised he would not suck dick without a condom. But he did. The more I thought about him, the angrier I became. In a fit of my own personal anger, I figured he deserved it. What a fucked-up way to feel. But he didn't ask for it. Nor did the other thousands of brothers and sisters who died. I felt ashamed of my feelings. I thought about the guys I knew who had died from this fucked-up thing. Seeing them suffer from debilitating diseases that changed the way they looked. The once beautiful and fine faces covered with lesions. Watching how they once pulled the men into their web of deceit; now they were the objects of repulsion. For whatever their reasons were, no one deserved it, not even him.

I was mad at myself for my thoughts. But I found myself even madder at the motherfucker who had done this to him, and to anyone else. His face was kind and his spirit was trusting. I figured the man he loved had betrayed him on so many levels. If he was equipped with the knowledge that the man he loved was infected, would he have protected himself? From his spirit at the party, I believed that he would have. There was a quiet innocence about him. Damn, those eyes. I saw him looking up at the asshole, slight tears in his eyes as the man he loved pumped death into him. He probably thought he was looking at love in his partner's face, but only death returned his glance.

As I continued to think of those eyes, I imagined they were looking at me. I saw them pleading to me. Silently telling me that he loved me. Softening my thrusts in him as I returned the look he searched for. I was his protector in this dream. I was the one there to make him smile again.

I spent the rest of the day chilling out and recuperating. I showered and thought of him. I ate, thinking about what it would be like to eat with him, sharing talk of our day with each other. When I finally took my ass back to bed, I thought of what it would be like to hold him. I grabbed my pillow as if it were him. I could smell his scent in the pillow. I breathed him in, taking in the freshness of his body. I felt the curve of his body as I held him close to mine. Holding him tight as my hands ran across what I am sure was smooth skin. Pressing my flesh into his without a spoken word between us and barely enough space to breathe or wriggle away from. He was mine, I told myself. He would be mine.

MARK

I played the voicemail messages as I prepared for work. I laughed at some of the voices blaring through the system, thanking me for a wonderful party. I could tell some of them had headed out afterward; I heard the music overshadowing their voices. The messages seemed endless. They were a mixture of joviality from the free food and booze, which I expected from some of the queens who showed up, to the genuine sincerity of friends who were happy that I was still there to receive their messages. I know, for a fact, my closest group of friends, those who were there at the beginning of this journey, were far more concerned than the party freeloaders. I even heard Mom's voice, gently shaking and praising God for me being alive. I stopped myself for a moment, taking in her message. She had been through a lot with me. She was a strong woman. Hell, she had to be, having a son like me. I wasn't always the angel she had hoped and dreamt for when she pushed me out of her womb. There was a lifetime of trials and tribulations. She was less than happy when I told her that I was gay. If someone could spit fire and burn you with their words, she could certainly do it. I sometimes thought she had taught gay me how to play the dozens with her cutting words. Eventually, she came around and realized I was still her son.

We became even closer when I had to tell her. I can't imagine what it was like for her. I had only taken my feelings into consideration. I am sure it killed her to know that her one and only son would die. She dipped into her motherly reservoir of love to shower me with reassurance that she would always be there. I couldn't dredge up those memories of letting her down as I got ready for work. I felt on the verge of tears thinking of her, but I couldn't go there. I made a mental note to give her a call once I arrived at work.

I stopped the messages long enough to take a shower. While I dried off, I pushed "play" once again for the remainder of what I assumed were more thank-yous and concerned calls. Then, I heard his voice.

I almost caught my dick in my zipper. I sat on the edge of the bed when I heard the deep richness of his voice saying hello. I listened as he thanked me for allowing him to be a part of the celebration of life. He stumbled over his words as he searched for the right things to say. I could feel it. He rambled a bit as he continued to share he'd had a good time. I chuckled a bit. I couldn't imagine why he would call. Come to think of it, when had I missed the call? As I continued to listen to his words, I smiled at his ramblings. He rushed to a conclusion, rattling off his number before he said he good-bye. I pushed the "save" button on the machine. I would once again replay his voice later that evening and retrieve the number. I checked the clock and noticed that I was running behind schedule. So I finished the last-minute prepping and took one final look in the mirror before heading out the door.

I was playing catch-up with the pile of work that had found its way on my desk from my time out of the office. It was pretty routine fare, but more than usual. I went about prioritizing the work at hand so not to overwhelm myself. I always am a bit out of sorts when I have a shit load of work to do, but I was still living and celebrating the party to get riled up. Not only that, but I was replaying his message in my head. I was wondering, after listening the first time, why he had called. I had found some scarves and gloves left over. After the message, I presumed they were perhaps left behind by him. However, after looking closely, they were much too small to accommodate his hands. I shrugged it off as I continued to comb through the stack of work.

The few co-workers I invited to the party made their way into my office to share their stories. The sisters who had attended were more than willing to share which brother they'd picked out they could "change back" from being gay. We laughed and because of our honest relationship, I reminded them that if they didn't have a dick and some chest hair, those brothers they longed after would only be good friends. One sister grabbed what was her imaginary manhood to show she was more than capable of doing the job. I had to tell her strap-ons didn't count.

As the clock ticked closer to the end of the day, I was some-what anxious to get home. Although I had ample time to rest from the party, I had worn myself out from the party and needed a little more sleep. It didn't help that the Sustiva I took nightly for the HIV still bothered me with its side effects. No matter how much sleep I got or attempted to get, I always woke up feeling less than rested. My doctor told me that I would have to deal with restless nights of tossing and turning. I sometimes would lie in bed after taking the medication, waiting for that one moment when I would sleep peacefully. I would drift off to sleep, my body tired from the day's activities, only to awake less than forty-five minutes later. This pattern would repeat itself throughout the course of the night, until the alarm would alert me of the six o'clock hour. I sometimes found myself avoiding the medications at night so I could get a good night's sleep; that was never a good thing. But when I did, I found myself well-rested and energized. I tried to avoid missing doses, for fear of building up a tolerance. Sometimes my body called for sleep more than it did the medication to save my life.

I decided when I got home I would take it easy. The place was clean and I still had leftovers from the party. I elected not to cook, but to toss something in the microwave for a quick fix. I took my clothes off and put on the ratty sweats that substituted for pajamas. I immediately pushed the "saved messages" button on the answering machine, and grabbed the pen and paper placed on the nightstand. Before I relaxed for the evening, I would give him a call to say hello and acknowledge his call. I didn't expect much from the conversation. Maybe I was hoping for something more, but I learned not to get my hopes up too high. After deciphering his jumbled message a couple of times, I got the seven numbers all in order. I retreated to the kitchen to eat before I made the call. The food was not as good reheated, but it served its purpose.

I grabbed a bottle of water from the fridge for the night's drug regimen and placed it on the nightstand. I turned the television on to have background sound. The level would be just enough to shift my attention if the call ran a little too long or didn't go the way I wanted to. I picked up the receiver and dialed.

KEVIN

I checked my pocket for the number that was given to me in the event I got lost on my way to the party. I knew D.C. like I knew the back of my hand, so there were no new sections or areas I didn't know about. His name and number was scribbled on a ripped piece of paper my buddy had given me, along with the address. There were many times I picked up the telephone and dialed a portion of the number before I stopped myself and hung up. I didn't know what I was going to say. How could I justify calling this man so early in the morning? I was granted a brief reprieve when his answering machine received the call. Instead of going with the lie I'd thought up about leaving something there, I only mumbled a thank-you for the invite and some shit like that. Before I knew it, I was leaving my number for him to give me a call. As I quickly hung up the telephone, I thought, *Why the fuck did I do that?* The answer was very simple indeed; I wanted to see him again. I hit the door running, still thinking about how much of an ass I sounded like with the message I had left.

I entered the office and saw the same folks from the previous week. I avoided some of them because they were too fucking nosey. I was out, but I chose not to let too many people into my private life. They knew it was a subject not to address. We would share the basics about weekend activities. Passing on our own reviews of movies—rated ones to see, but after shelling out the money weren't worth the time spent sitting in the movie theater. This was routine to me and I liked it that way.

After work, I decided to stop by the corner Chinese carryout for some wings and fried rice. It was the one place I could get wings, minus the hair from other takeout places, and that dreadful mambo sauce. I always kept a large bottle of Texas Pete hot sauce in the cupboard to drown the already tasty wings. I liked the kick it gave me when combined with the sometimes dry fried rice.

There was no need dirtying any dishes for this quick meal, so instead, I flipped open the lid of the Styrofoam container and grabbed the bottle of hot sauce. The one thing that burned my ass about the Chinese carryout was the lack of soy sauce they threw in the bag. They would give you more than enough of that nasty-ass hot mustard, which would later burn your asshole, but made you saddle up additional money for extra soy sauce. After being a patron of their fine establishment all this time, they still charged me. Sometimes I would say, fuck it, and head out the door. I would later find myself pissed and wishing that, instead of using the hot sauce, I had purchased the soy sauce. Well, you can't win them all.

The food contained the right amount of grease for my empty stomach. There was nothing better than chasing the meal with a cold Pepsi. I sat there alone, chomping on the wings, getting my eat on, in between using the Pepsi to cleanse my palate. I ate away like a man on death row, enjoying his last meal when I was interrupted by the telephone.

I grabbed one of the few napkins in the bag to wipe my mouth and hands before I reached for the wall phone. Before speaking, I waited a moment to ensure the chicken in my mouth would not get stuck and cause me to choke.

I cleared my throat and said, "Hello."

He responded in that gentle voice, "Good evening."

MARK

As I sat there Indian-style on my bed contemplating what to say, I heard his voice. In some way I felt like I was intruding on something since he seemed a little out of breath. I introduced myself, as if he didn't know who I was. For a moment, there was a brief pause as he apologized for his labored breathing. He informed me that he was eating and I felt bad for interrupting. He assured me it was okay. I was hoping at that moment he would say he would call me back. That would give me some time to come up with some decent conversation, versus searching for something to say. I listened as he rehashed the message he had left on the answering machine, thanking me for the invitation. But in actuality, now that I think about it, I didn't invite him. I didn't say anything. He was in control of the conversation at the moment, and it allowed me some time to formulate what I was going to say. When he stopped, I could hear him take a swig from the drink accompanying his meal; it was my cue to pick up the conversation. I informed him it was a surprise to hear from him. I let him know immediately that I wasn't sitting around thinking about him—although I had been since he had brushed his lips against my ear.

As we stumbled over each other to find conversation, I broke in, asking if he had left his gloves or scarf. I alerted him that I had found some unknown articles of clothing after the party. I figured that is why he had called. He surprised me by not missing a beat; he told me no and that he simply wanted to say hello.

My shoulders kind of sunk as I was hoping the lost garments would provide me an opportunity to see him again. I could return his items and see him in his full glory in the daylight. I continued to half-listen to his conversation, in between stealing glimpses of the news. He shared with me that this was the first time he had attended a party such as mine; he really didn't know what to say about it. By this time, a good deal of my attention had shifted toward the news. I figured he would say something stupid out of his mouth. I was used to getting calls like this. Sometimes you figure there is interest from someone when you hear their voice, when the real reason for the call is to ask a question about HIV. I really didn't want to deal with this shit this evening. I had spent the day waiting for this moment and it was going downhill. Everyone at the party knew I was positive; I was used to getting calls from friends, and sometimes strangers, to play HIV hotline operator. I would listen to the question, which was always disguised as, "Hey man, I have friend…," knowing good and damn well the friend in question was the person who had made the call. I prepared myself for such a conversation, feeling defeated and let down. I would answer, offer some telephone numbers for additional "crisis intervention," and hang up.

However, that didn't happen this time. I sensed the hesitation in his voice when he posed his question, "If you aren't busy, would you like to get together this weekend? Maybe grab something to eat?"

KEVIN

Before I could think of a proper way to say it, the words blurted out my mouth. I had been out on dates—some formal, some very informal; you know the "hit it and quit it" type. I always knew what I was getting myself into beforehand. Before I could figure where this was going or what I wanted, I had already opened the door for him to say yes or no. I knew in the back of my mind the reluctance that held me back; there was no need in lying. The fact that he was positive prevented me from asking him or treating him the way I would any other trick or date I was on the prowl for. I didn't want it to come across as pity for him, but I must have sounded like an asshole. I waited to hear that he was busy and unable to make it. That way I could say I was off the hook, no big loss. I didn't hear it.

I heard a sense of ambivalence and a bit of excitement when he said, "Sure."

I wasn't prepared for that. After playing it cool, we made plans to meet at Mr. Henry's on Capitol Hill that coming Saturday. Mr. Henry's was a local spot with no pretense. If we were lucky enough to grab a spot along the walls, we would be able to hear each other speak among the crowd that filtered there for the patty melts and onion rings. It was a happy medium between a flowers and candy date, and the bottle of wine and condom night. After a few more words, we said our good-byes and planned for seven p.m. Saturday night; not too early and certainly not too late.

I don't know why I felt proud of myself after I hung up the telephone. It wasn't like I had discovered some new equation to the laws of physics. I wasn't going to win an award for being Sensitive Man of the Year by asking a poz brother out on a date. No, there was nothing special about what I had done. There were others who had come before me and had done far more. They had given their heart and their love for people living with HIV. So why the fuck was I sitting here patting myself on the back? I guess I had taken pride in allowing myself to set aside some of my fears. I would at least find out more about this brother that captured my heart with his strength and the beauty of his eyes.

I made my way back to the kitchen table to eat the remains of the chicken and fried rice, grabbing another Pepsi to cool off the burning of my mouth from the heavy-handed hot sauce. I smiled as I picked up a wing and continued to enjoy what I had done.

MARK

I hung up the receiver, excited about the prospects of spending a few hours with this brother who, for a brief moment, sent my world and heart into a tailspin. I attempted to contain my excitement because I didn't know what to expect. I played out many thoughts in my head. Was he one who wanted to have the HIV expert conversation in person, rather than via a telephone conversation? There were some folks who would use an answering machine to record their conversations and play it back to their friends for fodder. Maybe he thought I was the type to do some childish shit like that. That wasn't my style. As much as I was comfortable with my status, the questions that friends asked because of their sexual behaviors stayed between the two of us. I wasn't really surprised by some of the things I heard when chatting on the telephone. Based on all the information that was available about how to decrease the risks of HIV disease, there were still folks having unprotected sex. One buddy called and was scared shitless after seeing blood in some guy's mouth that had sucked him off. I wasn't one to pass judgment because I had been there. Maybe Kevin wanted to ask some questions in person to convince himself some behavior he had engaged in was not only satisfying, but safe as well. On the other hand, I thought about the possibility that maybe he liked me. He saw something in me that many had seen in the past, but were afraid to follow through with because of me being positive. There were a handful who expressed interest in getting to know me, wanting to bed me down. Some even discussed taking it to the next level of possible love. But those thoughts quickly deteriorated after my revelation of my health issues. On occasion, it left me broken. I would kick myself after being honest and sharing the information needed to embrace the complete me. Sometimes it left me angry, knowing that a simple, yet complex, disease would prevent anyone from knowing the true me, and the love I had in my heart.

Whatever his reasons, I was going to seize this moment. It had been a while since I had gone out on a date. I needed, actually I craved, at the moment the chance to be someone's interest, whether it was for information or genuine attraction.

The television was a mere distraction as I envisioned what the date would be like. It was a few days away, but I immediately thought about what outfit to wear, made a mental note to get my hair cut that morning, so that I would have a fresh cut, and to eat something before we actually had dinner. I didn't want to appear greedy while sitting across from this man. I was not going to be a dainty queen and eat a salad, nor would I be the carnivore I could be. I placed my hands behind my head as I relaxed and thought of possibilities. It had been a while since I had allowed myself to think of a future with someone, after being told I was going to die. I hoped I wasn't placing the cart before the horse.

KEVIN

arrived a few minutes earlier to secure a nice quiet spot at Mr. Henry's. It was difficult to use *quiet* as a word to describe the setting. It was full of the usual suspects, consisting of the regulars who used it as a start to their evening. I suspected from the patrons, that some were there, much like me, for a blind date or to meet a trick for the evening. I found a nice little spot on the right side so that I could see Mark as he entered, as well as any of my boys who elected to stop by and check out the scene. It was as quiet as it was going to be for the evening; it allowed enough seclusion to not be spotted by the nosey asses that came in. For some reason, I found myself a little nervous. I ordered a drink to relax the tension I was feeling from Mark's pending arrival. I kept my eyes on the door as I watched the entrances and exits of the crowd. Tonight, the on-site manager decided to turn up the volume on the jukebox. The wails of the rock-tinged songs drowned out the conversations of those seeking a little anonymity. I let the drink calm my nerves as I looked over the menu. In all the times I had eaten here, there was nothing new added to the grease-stained menu. I could almost recite from memory all of the items available. I didn't want to rush to order so I placed the menu beside my drink as I waited for Mark. I played over in my head how the conversation might go. I wanted to stay away from intense topics and allow myself to enjoy the brother's company. But I was never one who was good for lighthearted conversation. I knew myself and my history; I was bound to say something out of left field. I took another sip of the drink and promised myself I wouldn't say anything stupid.

I continued to watch the door as I saw the white queens saunter up to the jukebox, dropping coin after coin. I was hoping they would play something a little more to my liking. I realized if I ventured there, my song choices would not benefit me, but the next patrons to grace the wooden seat I had fought to find comfort in. I checked my watch. I still had a few minutes before he would arrive. I noticed the old bitter queen with the big bulge in his pants. He was about as old as the restaurant itself. I didn't know for a fact whether he was racist or not, but in the past when I came here, he was always cold and distant to the black patrons. He would prominently display the thickness of his dick in the form-fitting jeans he wore when he was working. I guess he figured he would get bigger tips if he had something to offer the leering patrons that wasn't on the menu. I would notice how the eyes of hungry stomachs would find their way to his crotch, salivating for more than the onion rings and burgers. He was old, but he wasn't stupid. I guess, in these times, if you were lucky enough to make it this far in the game, you had to play the hand you were dealt. I am also sure he was able to pick up one or two who were willing to taste his wares. But, I realized looks can be very deceiving. The few white boys I hooked up with, who played the same game of display and conquer, were packing more balls than that bird. I laughed to myself and prayed that when I reached that age, God-willing, that I wouldn't be doing silly shit like that.

Finally, a song came on that I could hum and relate to; it helped distract me from the anticipation. As I found myself getting into the song, the door opened and there he was.

MARK

I went through every outfit that I had in my closet to find something to wear. Henry's was certainly not the place to wear a suit for an early evening dinner. For the most part, my closet consisted of the casual attire that many called preppy. When I did shop for casual Friday attire, I headed to the local Gap for khakis. I was one of a handful of brothers who suffered from the dreaded disease that plagued a select few in my community—nasitall. Translation, no ass at all. The only pants that gave me a semblance of curves were the white boy-inspired Gap jeans and khakis. It was cool enough for the evening to adorn a pair of jeans with a black turtleneck and a nice casual blazer. I had a shoe fetish, so I opted for the Kenneth Cole boots that gave me an extra inch in height. Hell, I wish it could have added inches to my ass as well, but the slight heel did provide a little lift to be seen. I tucked my freshly cut hair underneath a baseball cap as I braved the dropping temperature and made the few blocks walk to Henry's.

I was lucky to have found a nice place on Capitol Hill for dirt cheap, and it was great that it was in the heart of Eastern Market. If the weather was nice, I would be among the visitors to the weekend flea markets, checking out bargains and the numerous gay men and women alike. Every now and then, I was lucky to catch a few good bargains; if not, a few eyes from the pseudo-bohemian set now flocking to this part of town. I quickened my steps as I passed North Carolina Avenue past the park to meet Kevin for our "date." I started to second guess myself as each step brought me closer to Eastern Market and Pennsylvania Avenue. Am I overdressed or two casual? Should I have taken the time to comb my hair or was the baseball cap just right for a night like tonight? I thought about turning around and heading back home to go through the clothes that now littered my bedroom floor and change. Before I could make up my mind about returning home, I found myself at the front of the restaurant.

I could hear the music blaring from the jukebox before I entered. Fuck, I should have suggested another place along Pennsylvania to eat, rather than here. Every time I found myself here, I wound up shouting to those I was having lunch or dinner with, fighting the music and other meal seekers. Something told me this evening would be a bust. Rather than stand outside as the temperature continued to drop, I figured the evening would be over quickly. I could always retreat home and grab the pint of ice cream I kept in the back of the freezer to salvage such an evening.

I stepped aside as some of the regulars spilled out from an earlier happy hour, searching for taxis speeding down the street. White folks always enjoyed an opportunity to seize two-for-one specials here. On more than one occasion, after leaving, the liquor they consumed found its way back up on the side-walks; the heaving and chunks of broken fries leaving a nasty taste in their mouths and unsightly messes along the streets. I removed the baseball cap to let my curly hair breathe from its confinement. *Just like I thought, not too many of us here tonight.* But I really didn't care how many black faces were in the place;

I was only searching for one. And there it was, huddled in a corner, with a warming smile that took the chill off from the walk.

As I made my way over to the secluded booth, Mark stood up. He was taller than I remembered. I could tell from his choice of clothing that he had decided to go with the casual look as well. His jeans were not the baggy type many young men, or gay men, for that matter, had taken a liking to. Nor were they the tight ones used to draw attention to the size of a guy's dick when out on dates like this one. They were the perfect fit for a very perfect brother. As he extended his hand, I removed the gloves that warmed me during the walk. I was a bit nervous, and maybe some would say paranoid, when I extended my hand. In the years that I had taken the HIV medications, one of the side effects, was the deep-set brown streaks that graced my finger-nails. If you didn't look close enough to see the multi-brown hues, one would never notice. But as a person living with HIV, it was constantly a daily reminder of the disease running its course. After the initial handshake, I quickly removed my hand to place them gently in my blazer pocket, with the excuse of warming them.

I fought to get the attention of one of the waiters, hoping I wouldn't get the queen with the big dick. Let me stop, I must admit that I, like many others who have eaten here, have taken a glance or three at his crotch. It was something to behold, if I do say so myself. I had met white boys before who surprised me with the size of their dicks. But he, without pulling it out and laying it on the table, far surpassed the ones I had seen up close and personal. This time I wouldn't be afforded the opportunity to sneak a glance, as I watched him take the order of a group a number of booths down.

I decided against alcohol this early in the game, so I placed an order for a cup of tea to get the old blood circulating again. There was a bit of uneasiness as Mark and I stole looks, attempting to read the face of the other and to figure out what and how to begin the conversation.

We began with the general pleasantries that all dates begin with. We discussed for starters, the weather. We both agreed that this winter had been a little brutal, more so than usual, but were very happy that there was a brief respite from the chill. Topic number one was over. We moved on to topic number two, our careers.

Being in D.C., the "Chocolate City," as it was lovingly referred to, the number of gay brothers here were into job titles and the accumulated alphabets at the end of their names. Hanging out at the Mill, if you were asked your occupation and the answer was not suitable for the questioner, he would excuse himself. Then he would continue searching for the matching job and salary to complement his social standing in the community. It was a city of superficial queens. There were three basic questions that were asked by the game show host in order to secure a place in the winner's circle. Sometimes my answers got me to the semifinals, but never to the winning circle:

Question No. 1: Contestant, where do you live? My response, Capitol Hill. Good answer, good answer. Question No. 2: Contestant, what do you do for a living? Sometimes my answer was vague. I was able to think quickly enough to give an answer that was acceptable for the game master. Question No. 3: Contestant, what do you like to do sexually? What I found very interesting about this last question was the brazen boldness someone would have in asking such a question like that in a bar setting. I realized, after hearing it a number of times, that the answer one provided would either find you in a place with the questioner's dick in your mouth, or waiting for the next game show host to quiz you.

With these mini interviews of such, what I found disturbing the most was the one question brothers rarely, if at all, asked: Are you positive or negative? That was the one question that never drifted off the lips of these individuals as they sucked down the potent Mill drinks. HIV was certainly not at the top of their lists. The thought of getting some head, or even a piece of ass, was the most important thought. I found myself volunteering the information that was not given to me during the "game" I once played, only to be disqualified entirely.

Kevin and I continued to dance around conversations as we waited for the appetizers we ordered. I learned early on, not to divert my eyes from someone while listening. That was a sure indicator that you were not interested. As I listened to his voice, searching his entire face with my eyes, I realized I was in the winner's circle, simply by being here. He knew I was positive, so I was one step closer to winning the gold.

KEVIN

I can sometimes ramble on and on with conversation in comfortable surroundings. Sometimes my buddies would tell me to politely shut the fuck up as I fought to get my two cents in on every conversation. I had something to say about everything and everybody. Here, as I sat across from Mark, I sometimes found it difficult to engage in conversation. In this light, he was a pretty muthafucking man; there were no two ways about it. In my failed attempt at humor, and to break the ice, he would smile shyly and lower his head as if it were a silent apology for his behavior. I realized this brother had been beaten down a time or two. Whoever had fucked him over really had done a job on him.

In the few moments I had spent with him, I figured he was not the man dancing about at the party, showing the world how brave he was. No, he was merely an actor, conveying emotions he believed others wanted to see. In the moment, he appeared to be a chameleon of sorts. He was able to tap into the deepest thoughts of others around him, only to make them comfortable. If they accepted what was given or acted out by him, he was happy. Damn, this brother must have had to do this a while. I couldn't imagine playing a game like this to please others. My philosophy in life was, if you don't like what I say or do, fuck you. When he allowed me to see his face from hanging his head low,

I looked into his eyes again. I remembered the hurt I had seen, and it was seconded this time. It was at that moment, the fear I felt about his HIV status left. I wanted to know this man. I was no fucking savior, by any means, but I wanted to heal him. I couldn't take his disease away, but I could certainly try my damndest to heal his heart.

As the evening progressed and the conversation began to flow, I learned a lot about Mark—his favorite foods, movies, and music. I returned the information with my favorites as well. The wooden bench continued to bother my ass, but I embraced it as if it were a soft cushion. The tension from the earlier conversation slipped away. I blocked all side conversations from the patrons and focused solely on him. I noticed he became more comfortable as he decreased the number of times he lowered his head with laughter to disguise his insecurities. As we continued to get to know each other, we became the only two people in the world that mattered at that moment.

As he relaxed more, I saw his eyes brighten. He had now replaced the tea with a drink; his smile became wider with each passing word. He took careful note not to consume too much alcohol so not to slur his words. As he talked, I munched down on the grease-drenched onion rings, slathered with catsup. In between chews, I would ask a question in order to hear his response and enjoy the rings.

Everything was going well, until I asked the question I am sure he didn't want to answer this evening. Before I could reel it back in, it was too late. I stopped chewing. At that moment, I realized I had fucked up.

MARK

I lowered my drink to the table to catch my thoughts. What was going so well had now taken a turn for the worse. I saw myself contemplating the answer to the three questions I had answered in the clubs. But this time, I had to answer the question that he knew the answer to. Rather than give the pat answer of "yes, I am positive," this time I had to explain. No one had ever asked that question. *Hell, it was no one's fucking business*, I thought. I bit the bottom of my lip, wondering what the outcome would be after my answer; how quickly this evening would come to an end. I raised the glass to my lips to take a deeper swig this time, and inhaled a mighty deep breath.

I searched the rings of smoke drifting through Mr. Henry's for the starting point of the story. I raised my head, hoping to see some quick answer to the question and a quick exit from this conversation. But, there was no quick resolution to the question, or this moment. I grabbed the cigarettes from my blazer pocket— the pack I said I wouldn't smoke until the walk home after the date—but I needed something outside of the drink to take the sting away from the question. I inhaled the first puff of the smoke and lifted my head so not to blow smoke in his face. I watched as the answer to his question floated high above the two of us, searching for his sympathetic ear.

The story was a simple one. Boy moves to New York and falls

in love. Boy uses a condom initially with his love, only to remove it from the equation after hearing the words *I love you*. Boy begins to question boyfriend's infidelity. Boy tests positive. Simple enough, case closed, thank you, and come again. If the story was that easy to share, the moment would not seem so tentative. But there was more to the story that needed to be revealed for the first time.

I moved to New York City some twenty years ago with hopes of discovering myself. I was gay and hearing that New York City was the East Coast epicenter of gay life, I figured it was the place for me. San Francisco was clear on the other side of the country and too far away from my family. I wanted to have a comfortable distance from my family and loved ones, but close enough to take the first thing home in the event I was needed. I left with my family's reluctant blessing and an open-ended ticket to return to what I was used to. But once I got to the Big Apple, there was no turning back for me.

I felt I was in my element. Here was a city that nurtured and embraced the arts I so loved as a child. The first images of seeing the bright lights of Broadway were intoxicating and I drank it in. The Saturday subway rides to Harlem offered a chance to slip into the great days of the Harlem Renaissance. Smiling faces of proud black people crowded the streets leading to the famed doorway of the Apollo Theater. When the desire for good ol' Southern food outweighed the introduction to the numerous multicultural restaurants cluttering the city, Sylvia's gave me the feeling of sitting at Mom's kitchen table. But I found everything I needed and wanted in the Village.

On any given day, the Village gave me the sense of community I longed for when I realized and embraced the fact that I was gay. The numerous bars along Christopher Street became second homes to me after work. There on the bar stool, I met friends who became extended family members, the ones who could easily replace the dreaded cousins who made fun of my sexual orientation. They became the extended teachers of my thirst of knowledge to learn more about me as a gay man; the history of being gay in this mecca. The place where I laid my hat the most was Keller's. I noticed as I took another puff of my cigarette that Kevin was now into the journey. I had gone too far on this trip down memory lane to bring myself back into the moment. I continued to revisit the place that brought me both love, and pending death.

Keller's was always the joy at the end of Christopher Street. After checking in at the Monster for happy hour, heading toward the Pier, I would make my stops at the Hangar and Two Potato. Along the way, I would pick up friends who were interested in the trip; others only long enough to make their stops at their favorite watering hole.

At the corner of Christopher and West Side Highway, right before crossing the street to hit the Pier, was Keller's. From the outside, it was nothing to really brag about. As with any gay bar in New York, there was history that was overlooked by many. Originally connected to a hotel for sailors, Keller's transitioned into a gay bar catering to a predominately leather crowd. It eventually evolved into what I would refer to as the best place to hang out in the city.

Upon entering the lone door, and depending on the night, there were wall-to-wall black gay men—all ages, all shapes and sizes, all colors of a black rainbow, if there was such a thing. If you didn't arrive before the regular set, sitting at the bar was not an option for the evening. I would maneuver through the crowd to grab a drink and wait for friends, or just enjoy the house music that was all the rave, blasting from the corner jukebox.

One night, while waiting for friends who had a tendency to lie about meeting me out, I met him. We exchanged glances throughout the course of the evening. After checking the door, and my watch, a number of times, I realized I had been abandoned by friends. I decided to have one more drink for the road. As I made my easy to the bar, he was standing next to me. After polite conversation, we exchanged more than glances; we exchanged numbers. I had been in similar situations with guys I had met at Keller's. Sometimes an exchanged number turned into a date, or the once-too-often booty call; straight folks think all that gay men do is fuck. But, this brother was different.

Well, as the rest of the story goes, we hooked up. We started spending time together. I forgot all about the friends who constantly lied to me about meeting me. This time, I was the bearer of bad news and no-shows; I was with him.

As I was getting caught up in the story, I wanted to find a quick ending. It dredged up a lot of bad memories for me. So, I cut to the chase, for both my sake and Kevin's.

I fell in love with this man. When I wasn't at work, I was with him, and I thought the feeling was mutual. We became intimate and, as I always did, I used a condom each and every time I would allow him into me. There were no fears of HIV or sexually transmitted diseases. We were safe.

As I continued with the story, I began to realize how fucking stupid I was. I shared with Kevin how after a few months, this gentleman and I stopped using protection. I chalked it up to being young and in love. I figured since we were together morning, noon and night, there was no one else. The precautions I had taken as a gay man went out the window with a simple request of, "Can I take the condom off?" And I allowed him to do it.

I found myself on the edge of a cliff in my thoughts as I continued. As a gay man, I would incorporate getting tested as part of my annual physical. It was something I deemed necessary because of the lifestyle that had chosen me. Before moving to New York, I had tested negative. My sexual behavior was limited to the occasional jack-off or giving head reciprocally. Outside of this man, I had used a condom every time.

So, as you can imagine, I was surprised when I received the results from my doctor. I had waited a lifetime to be free, to be me, in a city that allowed me to live openly and honestly as a black gay man. It was only to have bad judgment take it all away. With thoughts of death, and lacking in the knowledge of what HIV was at the time, I told him. To say he was cold in receiving the information was an understatement. After numerous times of trying to see him after the test results, telling him was one of the last few times I heard from him.

I turned away as I felt my emotions begin to take hold of me, but I couldn't turn back. This was the first time I had allowed anyone into that dark moment of my life. All I could think of, as I turned my head toward the door, was hearing the operator say to me the number I had reached was now disconnected. I fought back fear and rejection. The place where we once made love in his apartment was now vacant, with no forwarding address. No one could tell me how fucking stupid I was as much as me. I spent the better time of getting hold of the disease looking for him and concerned about him.

I felt the trembling of my lip as I shared with Kevin the reaction of my family and friends. Some embraced the real me and offered love and support. Others were quick to tell me how foolish I was. Some friends stuck by me; others quickly took it as a way to cease communication.

I quickly ended the conversation by saying I was doing well. By my tone, he could tell I couldn't go on anymore. I refused to let one tear drop from my eyes as I revisited that time in my life. I swallowed the sobs that formed in my throat along with another sip of the drink. I had allowed myself to forget about it and him. I took another drag off my cigarette and waited for Kevin to do what "he" did. I waited for him to walk away.

KEVIN

I leaned back, after hearing what must have been some very difficult shit coming from Mark. He had proven my theory right about being hurt. I watched him as he looked for spots on the wall to stare at or focused his attention on folks coming and going in order to avoid making eye contact with me. From the side of his face, I could see the tears of telling me his story well up. I watched him as he took the burned cigarette to his lips to attempt one last puff and regain himself. I watched how twenty years of holding that shit in had taken a lot out of him. He butted his cigarette and returned to claim what was left in his drink. He pushed the now cold food aside and fidgeted with the cigarette pack for another Newport. I attempted to play mind reader, assuming my next move would rub salt in his freshly opened wounds. I only imagined he felt exhausted after spilling so much, but not as much as I was in hearing it. It was a mixture of anger and confused emotions. On one hand, I was mad at the muthafucker who had done this to him. If I was one of Mark's friends, I would have tracked him down and whipped his ass. On the flip side, my heart reached out to this man sitting across from me. It wasn't pity, by any means; it was a genuine concern for him and what he must have gone through. My observation led me to believe what I would say and what I would do next would make him feel that I understood, or that I pitied him.

Before he could bring the second cigarette to his lips, I reached for his hand. I felt how soft they were—not a hard day's work in his life. But they were scarred and calloused from the heavy burden he had carried. My touch signaled him to look at me silently. As he faced me, the tears that formed were now slowly running down his cheeks. While caressing his hand, I reached for the first of many tears. I smiled gently at him, welcoming him back from his long and arduous journey. With one touch of his cheek, and the words that followed, any fear I felt could not parallel the strength of this beautiful man who sat across from me.

I whispered loudly, so that not only he could hear, but for others who may have questioned my intent. "Do you know how beautiful you are?" And with that, the tears made way for the smile that I wanted.

MARK

I eventually pulled myself together in order to salvage the rest of the evening. When Kevin stroked my cheek, I felt a certain calm come over me. For the first time, outside of the numerous therapists I had seen over the years, I was able to let my guard down and take some stock in my responsibility for my own infection. In many ways, telling Kevin the who, what, where and why of my infection, empowered me. I had never allowed myself to be that vulnerable in front of anyone, let alone a first date. I was used to allowing my heart to continue to harden, never allowing anyone to penetrate the barrier I had built around my heart. Although I'd had a breakdown in front of him, I was able to claim a bit of me. No matter what happened from that moment, I was able to embrace that after all these years, I was positive. I didn't give a fuck what anybody thought.

I treasured the touch of his hand against my face. It was such a simple gesture but it meant a lot. We found ourselves out of this conversation, and moved on to much lighter fare. By the time we finished our meal, the restaurant had emptied itself of its patrons. That old queen had passed our table a number of times to silently tell us to get the fuck out. It was growing late anyway; I had to get home to take my medications for the night. I was pretty good at being on time with them, but I was lost in the magic of this time with him. It didn't matter.

During this time of night, I figured it would be difficult to hail a cab to get me back to my apartment. Once I stepped out into the cold air, I was not about to walk. I looked up and down Pennsylvania Avenue for the few cabs that would come to this part of town. It was only to have them pass me and pull up in front of the drunken partygoers of Remington's, the local country and western bar, a few doors down. Kevin followed closely behind, and we both bundled ourselves up. He told me not to worry about a ride since he was heading in my direction. We headed toward his car, and sat quietly as the engine hummed and the heater blasted to warm us.

As we pulled up to my front door, I knew my exiting the car would bring the evening to an end, but I didn't want it to be over. For the first time in a long time, I was having a good time on a date, and there were no expectations of me. We chatted a little more as a couple of cars sped through the streets, breaking our concentration. Underneath the street light, I could see Kevin's beautiful shadow. Under different circumstances, I would have invited him in, but I didn't want to tempt fate. I was hoping that he would extend an invitation to join me, but I didn't want to be a bit presumptuous. In one breath, I both thanked him for a wonderful evening and apologized for letting myself go at the dinner table. Once again, he reached over with his hand and rested it on mine. Apologies were not needed, he shared with me. He, in return, thanked me for my honesty. When I had found myself sharing only a small bit of my journey on past dates, I wouldn't get the response I received from him. Usually, it was the false promise of another date or a future call, but those promises never materialized. The date would usually drop me off and speed away to the next one. I would watch as the taillights faded in the distance, along with any hopes of seeing that person again, outside of running into them at a bar or club in the city. There would always be this uneasiness when seeing me—the stuttering conversation and attempts to find a reason to justify why they didn't follow up with a call. I always let them down easy when I found them searching for words.

With a reassuring hand, I would simply say, "It's cool, I understand." Only to cuss them out underneath my breath, when they walked away, the new face that had caught their attention earlier that evening.

As much as I wanted the evening to continue, it was time to get out. I dared not attempt to kiss him, as much as my lips longed for further touching from him. I said good night and thanked him. As I reached for the handle to exit, so did Kevin. He made his way around to my side of the car and stood there as I stood up. I was now facing his chest. We both paused for a moment, not sure of what to do next. Instead of the standard handshake, I felt his enormous arms wrap themselves around me. In the chilled air, I allowed myself to sink into his warmth. Damn, he felt good. He thanked me once again for a nice evening and watched as I made my way up the stairs to my place. I felt if I looked back, I would see the same taillights from past dates speeding away from me. So, I opted not to do that. I allowed myself to believe his eyes were safely watching me turn the key in the door and ensuring I made a safe entry into my home. Once inside, I quickly looked out of the window to see him still standing there. I closed the blinds and rested my back against the wall. In the darkness, I looked up to the ceiling, searching for the God who had made this evening possible.

I whispered, "Thank you, Lord."

KEVIN

I waited until Mark got in the house before I headed home. I watched as his body disappeared behind the door that now separated the two of us. In the past, I would have been walking behind brothers, knowing that I was going to get some ass, or maybe even a quick blow job to blow a nut before heading home. And truth be told, as much as the thought about fucking him entered my thoughts, I couldn't go there at the moment. Still lingering in the back of my thoughts was his status, but there was something special about him. Sure, I could have let the hormones take over and do a quick hit and run. But my heart told me, through all the reservations, that I wanted something a little more. Hell, I was getting too old to be throwing my dick around. I thought about my buddies who had hooked up and were now playing house with their boyfriends, or their pieces, for the moment. I was a little tired of playing the games. As I rode the now quiet streets of D.C., I thought about what it would be like to be able to walk behind the doors with Mark and not have to leave in the morning. I was kidding myself each time I saw the two of us in my thoughts, living a happy existence. I saw the images of us, getting up in the morning, roaming around "our" place and doing the morning breakfast thing as lovers do. I saw the two of us shopping together for things for "our home." I even allowed myself to see the images of the two of us making love. My dick started to get hard, but then it softened as I thought about the HIV. I replayed the story he had shared with me over dinner, wishing that the outcome of that test result would have been completely different. I knew if it were true, I would have been the one closing the door behind the two of us after dinner.

When I got home, I showered to warm up since I had turned the heat down before leaving for dinner earlier. I continued to think about Mark and found myself wondering what he was doing. As I lathered, my thoughts were brought back to the touch of his soft face. I will admit that of the other reasons I watched him enter his place was to check out his ass. He was one of the few brothers I knew that didn't possess a full set of ass cheeks, but it was enough to keep your eyes glued to what was there. The heat felt good as I imagined what his ass would feel like in my hands. I thought about the hug I had given him. I imagined that he had allowed me the pleasure of cupping his ass, as my hands slid down his waist. I started to get hard this time, and I allowed myself to run with the thoughts.

As the dream played out, I reached for my dick and stroked it ever so gently. Although he had a small ass, it was firm and full to the touch. With his arms stretching to reach around my neck and shoulders, I pulled him closer. I continued the stroking, feeling his ass in my thoughts, and building up to release in my reality. Now he was facing me, looking at me for silent instructions. I continued to beat my dick like it had stolen something as I leaned in to kiss him. He tasted the way I thought he would—a whiff of cigarette smoke, coupled with the faint taste of alcohol. The mints he sucked on before the kiss made me search his mouth deeper with my tongue. As I held onto his ass, he matched my kiss, tongue for tongue, lick for lick. I increased the movement on my dick, focusing only on his kiss and his taste. Before I knew it, I had busted nut all over the shower. I caught my breath as I let the water remove the sponge from my hand. I felt a bit guilty of thinking of him as a sexual object. But I traced his face with my thoughts of his beauty and let guilt follow the cum down the drain.

I lay in bed for a brief moment before fading out. I thought of Mark and what my next step would be. I already faced the reality that I wasn't going to let this one get away from me. I wanted to see how it would play out. As I closed my eyes, I knew my goal for the next morning would be to call again. I would see if he wanted to see me again; that's what I was hoping to do—see him again.

MARK

I sat at my makeshift desk, the kitchen table, going over some bills to pay and having morning coffee. I thought about the dinner with Kevin and how much I had enjoyed it. For a brief moment, I was hoping I would hear from him again. However, history had shown me brothers like him weren't really comfortable with guys like me. Oh, but for a brief—very brief moment—I thought about a future. It had been a long time since I had allowed myself to think about "what if's." What if he actually liked me? What if he loved me? What if we lived together? For years, I placed barriers around my heart, not only with dates, but with establishing friendships and pursuing any of the other goals I set up for myself. Along with the good "what if's," were the "what if's" that scared the shit out of me. What if I get sick? What if I am rejected? What if I fall in love and die? The thoughts smacked me back into reality as I played back my revelation to him. What if he runs away like the rest? The wonderful thoughts were now being pushed aside. I was shutting down again and thinking the worst. I was used to this.

Before I went down this path yet again, the telephone rang. I heard the voice on the other end and realized my fears were unwarranted. Kevin's voice prevented me from spending the rest of my day sulking and pondering the "what if's." After thanking each other for the previous night, he asked if I had some time that afternoon to walk around Eastern Market. I looked out the window to see the Sunday morning sunlight beaming through, as if to grant me a continued weekend of seeing Kevin. We agreed to meet for coffee at the local coffee shop before checking out the local vendors and artists that fought for space during the weekend. Pushing aside the bills that had accumulated, I quickly showered and looked at the clothes littering the floor from the previous night. I grabbed a pair of jeans, ran the iron over them and then picked up a sweater. I had allowed my hair to grow out, so it was a bitch to completely dry without damaging it with a blow-dryer. I grabbed yet another baseball cap and pushed the curls underneath, as much as I could, before checking myself in the mirror. I okayed what the end result was and headed out the door.

The same route I took heading toward Mr. Henry's was the same route I had traveled to meet Kevin for coffee. This time, the empty streets were now replaced with vendors and peddlers selling their wares. The streets were crowded with locals and others searching for bargains from homemade desserts to replicated original works of art. If my schedule permitted, I usually rummaged through the bins of local record collectors, searching for an original vinyl recording of Nancy Wilson that I didn't own. I could spend hours going album by album, crate by crate, searching for something with her name on it. Her Capitol Records recordings were difficult to find, but if I stumbled across one that I didn't have, I splurged and treated myself. If nothing was found, I would still pick up something that caught my interest—an old Pearl Bailey recording or my other favorite, Dinah Washington. I learned early on, if you didn't waste the vendor's time and occupy too much space seeking a specific recording, any purchase of their items would go a long way in the future. Once you became a staple, it was easy to ask them to hold on to what you really wanted until your next venture out. But, I didn't have time to do that right now. With kids in tow, many of the patrons blocked my way in trying to get to the coffee shop. As I walked around kids begging parents for this item and that one, my patience began to wear thin. I wanted to tell these mothers to move their damn kids out of the way.

I finally made my way through the crowded street to see Kevin standing with one hand in his pocket, the other holding tightly a carrying tray of two cups of coffee. He must have noticed me as well because I noticed his smile broaden with each step I took. He motioned the coffee toward me and informed me it was black, since he didn't know what I liked added. After dashing into the coffee shop to doctor the coffee with cream and Sweet'N Low, we made our way out the door and through the open-air market.

We walked around, taking in the sights and conversing. On occasion, we would stop at a booth or two while the other looked around for something to pick up. I didn't want to spend the majority of my time going through the albums that I searched through on a regular basis. So, I selected something quickly and thanked the vendor. He reminded me that he was still looking for Nancy Wilson albums for me; to check back with him in a couple of weeks. As we continued to make our way from one side of the market to the other, Kevin and I continued to share laughs and smiles.

We agreed to grab something light to eat for lunch inside the market. I hadn't had fish in a long time and decided on a quick fish sandwich at one of the outlets. I was enjoying the moment, as I hoped he was as well. Before I had left home, I had promised myself that I wouldn't allow the conversation to veer into sensitive territory. I would go with the flow and enjoy his company.

We lost all track of time spending the day together. The crowds were now thinning out and because of the time, we were losing what was left of sunlight. There was a moment when I thought about inviting him over since I lived so close by, but I didn't want to rush anything. He made no attempts to make any suggestions either. With our purchases in hand, we embraced before saying good-bye. As I made my way home, I was happy to have spent some additional time together with him, but uncertain of his motives. However, I said to myself, whatever they were, for a brief moment, I didn't care. I allowed myself to just be in the moment.

KEVIN

I didn't usually follow up so quickly with someone after a date or spending time. I would play the game to see who would call the other first. If I didn't hear from them in a couple of days or so, it wasn't worth my time. Now if they contacted me immediately, I was in control of the game. The ball was in my court and whether there was interest or not, they had granted me the permission to get in that ass. It was the desperation I heard or sensed in their voices. Yes, I had mastered the game of wooing brothers to get what I needed. I didn't have to go out of my way to make the seduction elaborate. No, it was in my actions, the use of my words, and the attention I made them think they were getting. But here, Mark was changing things up on me.

After those two dates, I found myself chasing him. I would pick up the telephone at all times during the day and evening to check in on him. I hoped that, at some point, he would reciprocate the calls, but he played his cards close to his chest very well. I was easier to read when talking with him. I made small talk just so I could hear his voice and see how his day was going. At times, we would arrange moments to get together and have a drink or dinner. Once or twice, we checked out a movie; I was always close to the door, but never inside to see his world. I sensed there was an interest on his part. He never gave me any signs to discontinue my calls or occasional meetings. There was

nothing written in stone between the two of us. As each telephone call grew longer, each date leading to another, I developed
some feelings for him. If he felt the same way, he never showed
it. I was used to brothers revealing their feelings immediately; I
could determine if it was something I wanted to pursue.

When I couldn't get him on the telephone, or the call went
directly to the answering machine, I must admit I thought the
very worst. I started to become a little paranoid, thinking that
he was rushed to the emergency room, or his medications were
fucking with him, as he once told me. As I paced the floor, thinking of driving over to check on him, his call would interrupt this
overprotected spirit and let me know he was okay. I needed to
put this shit in check. After those first couple of dates, I realized
that I wanted him in my life, but to what extent was still puzzling
to me. I didn't want to be the protector of his reality. I didn't
want to come across as being too focused on the bad things
that would or could happen to me, but focus on possibilities with
him. During our conversations, we briefly touched on the subject of his ailment. I didn't want to call it a sickness; that would
give it too much power. In between conversations, I read about
HIV to become more educated on how to cope and deal with him.
I promised myself that I would not pity him. If he felt that, I would
get a little of his shit—thinly disguised by his Southern charm.

When I looked at him over dinner, or watched him as he inter-
acted with others, I saw a man with a disease; not a diseased
man. For all outward appearances, he was healthy. He didn't look
like the images that once ravaged our community as gay men,
both black and white. In talks with friends who were in relationships or who had dated positive brothers, they likened HIV to
being a nuisance more so than anything else. They shared with
me how they treated it like the friend who wouldn't leave when

you wanted him to. Sure, you couldn't do things that you once did carelessly before HIV. But the joys of exploring the depths of someone's heart and soul in the process far outweighed cumming in someone's mouth or ass. I didn't have to take their words for it; I saw how they treated their boyfriends, or fuck buddies, who were positive. There was this mutual respect to protect and enjoy one another. Sure, when they got pissed they still said, "fuck you," and "kiss my ass," to one another. But, it was silently agreed upon that you would not and could not go there in pulling the HIV card.

I still dealt with the fear factor, not of becoming infected when it concerned Mark. Hell, we hadn't even kissed, and for me, this was a first. I like to get a nut just like the next man, but I waited patiently for Mark to give me a signal that I could even cross that line with him. Our evenings usually ended with a longing hug and me rushing home to jack my dick. I will admit, if Mark were negative, and we continued to play this game of cat and mouse, I would have reached out to an old piece of ass just to get my rocks off. I would keep it as a booty call, while still pursuing Mark. But, for the life of me, I couldn't do that to him. He had struck a chord in my heart that very few had even come close to doing. I wanted to try the concept of monogamy with this brother, even if what we were doing was not truly defined. I went with the flow and expected nothing in return. I was simply happy he was generous with his time and was patient with me.

MARK

There were very few calls I looked forward to receiving. Outside of my mother and the few close friends who stuck with me through some of the most difficult times, I didn't really care for the telephone. I guess after receiving calls from past lovers, shady friends, and friends of friends, to share the name of yet another brother who had died, was more than I could take. As of late I had become the recipient of Kevin's calls. Initially, I didn't think much of them, but as time passed, I found myself late at night listening to his voice. There were times I would let the answering machine pick up his calls; I didn't want to appear to be too anxious. We had been spending a good deal of time together, learning each other, and enjoying each other's company. It was great to have the knowledge that, although it was unspoken, there was some interest on his part. But I had been here a couple of times over the last twenty years. The calls started out in abundance, pretty much the same as Kevin's. The guys knew of my status as well, but after thinking that their interest would go further and having given up the ass, I was left with calls that were placed on my part and never returned. I sometimes felt less than after these encounters. I would have respected the guys more if they had said they just wanted to fuck, and left it at that. But no, I fell right into their traps. One would think I would have learned my lesson by now, but I used my status as a crutch. Just the mere thought someone would be interested in me was a good feeling, regardless of how it ended. I wound up looking like an ass, and a little harder, to anyone who came down the pike bearing false promises.

I guess that's why I questioned Kevin. If he wanted to hit it, I would have gladly given in, since I thought about him in a sexual manner anyway.

On the occasions that Kevin and I spent time at each other's place, we would just lay there, watching something on television, his arms wrapped around me and my back pressed against his body. With the slightest movement or adjustment to make myself more comfortable, I would brush against his crotch. I could tell he was aroused; hell, I felt it hit me in my back. But, each time I attempted or entertained the thought of touching him in a loving way or to show that I was certainly interested in what he had to offer, he would maneuver my body away from his growing erection and pull away. He would chalk it up to being caught up in the movie or television show we were watching. I would refocus my attention to the screen, feeling somewhat rejected.

We could nip all of this in the bud if that's all he wanted. We weren't officially dating, and I presumed he had others he spent time with. I questioned where this was going. I found it difficult to believe he had time for anyone else outside of the calls that filled my answering machine and the times we spent together—whether in person, or at night on the telephone.

Those late-night calls turned into incoherent conversations; a result of the medications. Early on, during one of our chats, I had to inform Kevin about the side effects I was experiencing. I went on and on one night, not making any sense. I had had this feeling before of feeling "high" from the medications, and had friends question me during conversations if I were high or drunk. I came across as being loopy and fighting for control of the words that came out of my mouth. Rather than make me feel bad for these moments that weren't in my control, he allowed me to ramble. He would decipher on his own what I actually meant to say.

I wasn't spending nearly enough time on the telephone with the few friends in my circle. On the rare occasions they did reach me, I was constantly quizzed about who was taking up my time. If I happened to be on the phone with Kevin, I would click over the call waiting and quickly say I would get back to the caller, only to lie to myself and them. I would continue the conversation with Kevin until we were both exhausted, or my tongue began to feel thick from the drug haze.

I eventually had to confess to one friend what was going on. I didn't mention Kevin's name because he knew Kevin. I refused to reveal this information for fear of jinxing what was happening. I shared what I wanted, to his exasperated voice.

Even the evenings Kevin and I had dinner or ventured to a movie, I found out-of-the-way places versus the usual locations for gatherings. I knew how sissies were. I had been the unwilling victim of their fucked-up ways. There was one time I had a friend visiting me from my hometown. He was a new face in the crowd, so upon entering the bar, everyone turned to see who he was and fought their way to get his attention. He was grown, and it really was none of my business who he was fucking or who was fucking him. But there was always one little loose-lip queen who would take joy in the few minutes he granted them on the dance floor to reveal that I was HIV-positive, whether they knew for a fact or not. It even happened with dates. I got to the point if I was talking to someone and I slipped this information into our conversation, all eyes would seem to focus on what the fuck I was doing. For the life of me, I didn't understand sissy shit like that. It seemed they felt they needed to share my HIV status with others, before I did or felt it was time to do it. It was always one little bitch in the crowd who felt they needed to save a date or dance partner from becoming infected, just by being in my presence. For whatever selfish reasons they had, they took joy in beating me to the punch sometimes.

Since I didn't drive and relied on public transportation, Kevin's car became my transporter to faraway lands like the suburbs of Northern Virginia and Maryland. It was safe to go to these areas and enjoy this time without being surrounded by peering eyes. We would sit in his car sometimes, talking before saying our good-byes until he rushed home to call me. As horny as I was, this was a blessing to both of us, especially since the last few times I had invited him in, I felt him harden against me while we lay watching a movie.

I put no high expectations on the events that had been taking place over the last few weeks Kevin and I had spent together. I was getting to know him, and I opened up to allow him to get to know me. If nothing came out of what we were doing, at the very least, I could say I had a new friend. It was the first time in a long time I had allowed myself to start something I possibly could never finish. If nothing developed, I wouldn't have to save face by telling friends he was no longer in the picture; that's why I refused to divulge his name.

Even as things seemed in sync, and were going right for me for the first time in a long while, as always, Kevin showed himself to be just like the others.

KEVIN

I didn't feel like I was wasting my time with Mark, but the waiting was getting a bit much for me. I enjoyed our conversations and get-togethers, but I wanted a little more. The urge to fuck was getting the best of me, and although I was feeling him, there was still that block there. Jacking off became old hat, even though I enjoyed feeling my own dick. But I wanted someone else to take matters in hand. There were times I would feel him in my arms, lying on the sofa watching television. As I mentioned before, he didn't have a big ass like some of the brothers I had been with, but it was ample enough for the tapping. Because I held him so tight, he would wriggle in my arms, pressing his ass up against me. I would fight an erection each time this happened, but it was a losing battle. I sensed that he wanted more, and if he was anybody else, I would have given in to temptation. I felt bad lying to him, always telling him I was really into the show, now the last thing I was interested in. I wanted to be in him, but fear continued to kick me in the ass. He never really expressed any disappointment, but his body language told me what he couldn't. He would drive a wedge between the two of as he backed away, giving me too much space between the two of us. He was a damn good pretender. He never showed any signs that he was upset, but I did feel a distance between us.

I figured if I stepped out of this thing we were doing for a moment, no one would have to know, especially Mark. We were used to getting together on weekends for dinner and hanging out, but I needed to get some ass soon.

I decided to break from tradition of our dinners and conversation. I called and left a message for him, knowing he would not be home, and it gave me a chance to do so without feeling guilty. What I was about to do was fucked up, but emotions and the need for closeness of another body were getting the best of me. I figured by leaving a message to reschedule for getting together later that weekend, I would ease any possibilities of disappointment in his voice and ease my guilty conscience.

After work, I headed down to the Fireplace to get my drink on. As usual, the place was packed with wall-to-wall brothers, huddled together to cop a quick feel or generate just enough body friction to make a brother's dick hard. I was able to grab a drink after waiting in line for a bit, hovering the drink above my head so the local drunks would not force me to spill it by bumping into me. The music was pumping loud as I cruised the cramped quarters upstairs. It had been a few months since I had ventured out alone, or I wasn't with Mark. I saw the regular barflies, who were permanent fixtures after a long work week. From across the crowded room, I raised my drink to acknowledge them, but kept a safe distance since I was on the hunt. I stood close enough to the stairs to stake out the faces of those who wore form-fitting shirts over their gym, worked-out bodies. It would have been one thing if they were doing it for themselves, but it was for those they sought to catch for the evening. I was guilty of doing the same shit and playing the same game. I didn't focus so much of putting my chest out there, but tonight, I decided not to wear underwear. Those whom I brushed up against or would later dance with would feel the thickness of what was in my jeans. I grabbed another drink and left a tip for the bartender, who had hooked me up with the top-shelf shit, instead of rail liquor. He took care of me and I, of course, returned the favor. There was nothing worse than pissing off the guy pouring your shit. He would certainly remember the next time you requested something.

I continued to look around as I swallowed my second drink. Although I liked the Fireplace, I knew I would eventually end up at the Mill, so I drank in moderation. As I thought about heading over to the Mill, I felt sucker punched. Mark didn't live too far from there, and here I was out on the prowl. Guilt continued to weigh heavily on me as I thought of the bitch way I had left a message canceling the evening. That's why my punk ass was alone. I thought about the string of guys I had done this to; I started kicking myself in the ass for doing it to Mark. I felt even worse as this fine brother walked up the stairs and caught my eye. It was crowded, I readily admit, and he had more than enough room to make his way past me. But playing the game that we all play, he backed his ass against my free-balling dick long enough to leave an impression. He looked back at me to excuse himself, but he knew what he was doing. Instead of getting off of me, he pushed back more to let someone pass him. I could have easily gotten in his ass, but I didn't want to jump the gun this quick in the evening. I would then rush home afterward with the guilt I was feeling, and take the hottest shower to absolve myself of this sin I contemplated.

I finished the drink, politely pushed this brother off of me, and headed to the Mill.

MARK

It was only a matter of time, I thought, as I played the message over and over. I was pissed off and hurt, and shook my head. I was used to spending these Fridays with Kevin, whether it was eating dinner or talking on the telephone. All I had now was a message left informing me that he was unable to get together. I continued to push "play" to hear the message and the rapidness in his voice to leave the message and get out of our plans. I sat there thinking how glad I was that I hadn't told anyone his name. Yet I was upset that I had even shared with my friends that I was interested in this nameless man. I was jumping the gun with my thoughts that he was with someone else. For a brief moment, I wished beyond wishes that something had happened that prevented him from getting together with me. But I had heard that tone of voice before, so I knew instantly there was no emergency. I played the message once again as I decided to be reckless in my thoughts and actions.

There is always that one good, good "Judy," that loves to hit the streets at the mere suggestion. I thought about who would be willing to hit the bricks with me to "ho" for the evening. It wasn't like there were many to choose from, but I called my "Judy," to plan the rest of our evening. Once we confirmed the time of pick-up, I went about the task of getting my shit together. I never missed getting my hair trimmed and lined weekly because

I prided myself on looking good. Spending the extra money for getting my mustache and goatee trimmed was a small investment. I decided on the outfit for the evening prior to showering the freshly trimmed hair and softening the skin for a much closer shave. Anger continued to take over me as I scrubbed my body and replayed the message over in my head. I carefully shaved the stubble left behind by my barber's razor so not to cut myself. After drying off, I reached for the form-fitting boxers that gave me a sense that I had an ass. They hit what few curves were there, providing a false sense of fullness for me and those I planned to play games with this evening. I opted against putting on a baseball cap. Naw, I had spent the time making sure each hair was in place, every curl capturing the light from a different angle. I reached for the lotion to provide that glow underneath the harsh strobe lights, which I would be under in a matter of minutes. It served two-fold as I ran my fingers along the neatly trimmed mustache and goatee to make sure every hair was in place. I opened the medicine cabinet to pick the perfect scent from my favorite bottles of cologne. Anger had driven me to pretty myself for the evening, all the while hurting inside for something, someone—Kevin.

As I waited for my ride, I poured a shot of tequila that I kept in the back of the kitchen cabinet. When I was really pissed or hurting, the tequila became the friend I sought out for moments to console me. It burned like hell going down, but it didn't stop me from taking one more. I heard the horn blow from outside. I wasn't a vain bitch, but a while ago, I had purchased a three-quarter-length mirror that hung outside the closet door from where I retrieved my coat. I checked myself carefully in the mirror. I wanted to make sure my shit was right. Tonight, I felt like I had gotten played by Kevin.

KEVIN

The Mill was packed as usual. The line wasn't as long this evening, but as I paid to get in, I could see from the front door that the dance floor was packed. Before heading there, I ventured upstairs to check out what was happening. I don't know why motherfuckers always interrupt what they are doing, or what they are saying, when they hear that door open to the top level. I guess it breaks their attention and focus when they hear the heavy bass line intrude on what they are doing, or intending to do. I saw some of the brothers I had avoided in the past, giving that "fuck you" look because I hadn't returned a call. The one thing I liked about the upstairs at the Mill was that you could actually see faces, not try to make heads or tails of what someone looked like before the houselights came up. With the downstairs lighting, you could spend an evening chatting someone up, only to realize at last call, when the bright lights came on, that you wouldn't fuck them with someone else's dick. Here the lights were softer and gave you enough of a clue of what you were getting into. I grabbed a beer from the bar, rather than my usual. Mill drinks had a way of fucking you up way too early in the evening. I lucked up and found an empty stool and then turned in the direction of the pool table to check out who was playing. It was one of the safest things to do up here; either watch the pool hustlers, or walk to the back. There you'd hear the loud thumping of Bid Whist and Spades games; listening to the old girls talking shit after running a Boston. The music here was low enough to understand and sing along with, but it also allowed you an opportunity to eavesdrop on conversations. Sometimes you could hear the shit of some brothers bragging about how they were going to tear someone's ass up, or some queens going through drama because the pieces they had left with the previous night had stolen their wallets. Sometimes I laughed at shit like this. Sometimes I was guilty of participating in conversations like this. But this time, I was torn between my desire to fuck, and my desire to be with Mark.

After a few songs on the jukebox, I headed downstairs for a dance and a drink. I exchanged glances and hellos with brothers heading upstairs as their eyes immediately went to my crotch. Subtlety wasn't strong here. As I got to the bottom step, I sidestepped the piss that was now overflowing from the restroom. It seemed like every time I came here, I left with the smell of piss on my shoes. Luckily, this time, it didn't take over the entire walkway.

Heading to the dance floor, you were always subject to pass the aging bar owner. For some, she was a surrogate mother, granting them the freedom to be themselves in a place that provided an outlet for their gayness. It was as if she were the fairy godmother to everyone there. She greeted all with a smile as it became more and more crooked from the drinks she consumed throughout the course of the evening. The guilt I felt was subsiding with each sip of the beer in my hand.

I could tell the deejay was in a good mood, bumping some serious-ass music. Everyone was on the dance floor working shit out; whether it was sexual frustration, or the end of a long work week, the kids were having fun. The beer got me going as my head started moving along to the beat. My eyes darted across the crowd, searching the twisted faces of desire and lust. The music was their aphrodisiac. Just like the Fireplace, there were an abundance of queens faking their backs up to feel what they desired as well. I played the game and gave them a sample of what they could get, if the mood hit me. At that moment, this cute little brother asked me to dance. Feeling no pain from the beer, we headed out to the floor to make our way through the restless natives, shouting and carrying on. This brother reminded me of Mark, but not as cute. His body type mimicked Mark's as he backed his ass up against me on the dance floor. I closed my eyes, thinking about the message I had left. For a moment, it felt like Mark was with me in the form of this queen before me. He was doing for me what I wished Mark could've done at that moment. I closed my eyes and fantasized about a dream yet to come true.

MARK

My patience was running thin as we searched for a parking space close and safe enough to the Mill. The thought of cutting loose the bullshit and time I spent with Kevin was my driving force this evening. After this bastard, I would never allow someone that close to my heart again. I would become a bitter old queen, playing the games we played, avoiding any semblance of closeness to anyone leading me to believe there was something there. After squeezing into a tight parking spot, I lowered the visor and applied a light coating of ChapStick to my lips. I folded a piece of gum into my mouth. Someone was going to kiss me tonight, you could best believe that. We bundled up and headed to the short line waiting to get in.

After paying the admission, I made my way to the coat check and left my coat in the attendant's care. I was on a mission. My "Judy's" only thought was that we were out to have a good time, oblivious to the pain I was feeling from being ditched for the evening. I bee-lined to the bar to grab a drink to complement the two shots of tequila I had swallowed before arriving. I wanted to keep the buzz going; I was in a self-destructive mood tonight. Before I faced the dance floor, I took two big gulps of the drink, which burned more than the tequila. I wanted it to hit me like a ton of bricks, giving me the courage I felt I needed to play out this game tonight. I checked both ends of the bar to see who would be the first, second, or third conquest I would go for. After scoping out my prey, I hit the drink again and began the dance.

I really didn't care what he looked like as I approached him. I noticed he was checking me out when I ordered my drink. I decided, for the night, that he would do for what I needed. I extended my hand and said hello. I looked around to see what other prospects I could line up as he inquired in my ear if I wanted to dance. I didn't really like dancing at the Mill. It was always crowded, and tonight was no exception. Every now and then, someone would take a drink on the dance floor, and in the euphoria of dancing, would spill shit either on my clothes or shoes. I looked out to the dance floor to see what I had to fight against to make my way onto the floor. I spotted Kevin.

The anger I felt after hearing his message was magnified as I saw him humping on this brother's ass. My newfound companion waited patiently as I shook my head yes to his request to dance. Part of me wanted to go over to Kevin and create a scene. The alcohol had given me the courage to show out, but I took a sip and planned out my next move.

Now I know it is childish and stupid to play games, but I felt like the time I had spent with him and getting to know him was a game to him. I had opened up and gotten the shaft. With each step toward the dance floor, I watched him grind on that motherfucker's ass, never once suspecting that I was there. I swallowed the remains of the drink and placed it on one of the few tables surrounding the dance floor. The brother, who was now my dance partner, moved closer to me, with barely enough room for me to breathe. The alcohol was going full throttle as I welcomed this brother's advances. He was of solid build and attractive enough to serve his role well this evening. As soon as

I got my groove going, with the latest house music blaring from all corners of the cramped floor, the deejay threw in some old school house. I closed my eyes, turning away from the brother and allowing him to explore my backside.

I felt his left arm grab me around my waist, drawing me closer to him. I lost my footing but managed to regain it quickly as he became my support. With my eyes closed, I felt him slowly and rhythmically grind into my ass. It felt good, but it was missing the one thing that all these dances had a tendency to lack: the sincerity I wanted. I thought to myself if I hadn't waited so long to give Kevin the go-ahead to try something, or the permission to hold me, maybe he could have been the one with his arms around me. I opened my eyes and caught a glimpse of Kevin staring at me. He was still on the dance floor as the queen was now facing him in search of some frontal bump and grind. His blank stare didn't move me as I returned the glance and continued, although hatefully, enjoying the touch I longed for.

The music changed yet again and I was tired of being bumped into and moved by those flooding the dance floor. I thanked my dance partner and made my way to the bar again. My "Judy" came up and pointed out Kevin to me. He reminded me that Kevin had attended my Celebration of Life party. I played it off because I didn't want to give any indication that I remembered him, or that he was the one whom I spoke so favorably about the last few times we had chatted. By this time, Kevin and that little bitch were off the dance floor. He kept his eyes focused on me as the one interested in him stood and tiptoed to whisper something in his ear, all the while discreetly slipping his number in Kevin's hand. I wasn't going to stand around to see how it played out. I signaled to my buddy I was heading upstairs to cool off for a bit and passed Kevin as I headed toward the staircase.

I nodded in his direction hello and kept pressing forward. I was jealous to see him continuing this conversation in front of me, but I refused to let him see how upset I was. As I headed up the stairs to save face and grab another drink, I felt Kevin's eyes follow me. He noticed that my dance partner from earlier was now behind me, quickly on my heels. Something in my gut told me to turn around, and I followed that instinct. I glanced over my shoulder to see Kevin's spot empty. I heard my dance partner call out to me, but all I could hear in my head, was my voice telling me how I had fucked this up.

I was quiet on the short ride to my house. My head felt like someone was hitting me with crab mallets. All I wanted to do was get home and get something in my stomach to prevent what I was sure to be a morning of vomiting and nausea. I didn't let on to my buddy what had happened. Then he would have wanted to stay up the rest of the night being nosey. I stumbled to the door, searching for the key to get in and thinking about this fucked-up night.

Less than five minutes later, the doorbell rang. I presumed it was my ride to the club wanting to use the bathroom before heading to the Delta to continue his night of partying. As I stumbled to the door to unlock it, much to my surprise and anger, it was Kevin.

KEVIN

I took the piece of paper with his number scribbled on it and threw it out the window as I got in my car. I was mad at shit. I sat there with the heater blowing, pissed off at the bullshit that had taken place in a matter of minutes. I hit the steering wheel, knowing as much as I was mad with Mark, I had no one to blame but me. I had come out looking for something that I could have easily gotten from Mark. But I couldn't allow myself to go there with him. I couldn't see fucking him, as much as I wanted to since I had first seen him. Yet I couldn't imagine that motherfucker he danced with doing it either. I had some fucked-up double standards. I was the one who had put the ball in play by canceling at the last minute. But I didn't like the outcome of seeing someone all over him. I put the car in gear and headed home, but found myself heading up Eighth Street to make the turn onto Maryland Avenue to camp out in front of Mark's.

I sat there asking myself, what the fuck was I doing? I found a parking spot a few doors up from his house and waited to see what time he would show up. I convinced myself that I was concerned because of what I had seen him drink. In reality, I wanted to see if he was that pissed and hurt with me to bring that brother back here.

A few minutes had passed before I saw an unfamiliar car pull up to his door in my rearview mirror. There were no other available parking spots on the street. I noticed the car had no intentions of staying for a while. I waited long enough to see him slowly enter his place before I cut off the ignition to follow him.

The few steps it took me to get to the door didn't give me enough time to come up with something to say. The hostility I felt was easy to read on my face. When he opened the door, he must have presumed, before looking up at me, that it was his driver. I could smell the mix of alcohol on his breath as he tried to make heads or tails of who I was.

I looked at him, wanting to shake the shit out of him; I was jealous. I didn't allow him the pleasure of telling me that I needed to leave as I pushed my way into the door. I looked around, checking to make sure no one was present before I started in on him.

I shook my head as I lashed into his childish behavior. He knew that I had seen him pushing up on the brother on the dance floor. As I continued, I never once acknowledged that I was at fault for his actions that evening. I didn't even bring up the boy who was riding my dick on the dance floor; right now, it wasn't about me. It was about him. I would not allow him to get a word in. I looked at him, sobering up from the words I used to penetrate his heart and thoughts. I was so fucking mad I wanted to hit him. Sad as it may sound, I knew at that moment I loved this man. I threw every harsh word at him to break his spirit, to see him ball up and cry, but he didn't give me the satisfaction.

MARK

I avoided the easy chair in my path as I headed to the closet to hang up my coat. All the while Kevin's words hit me in the back of my neck with such force and venom. I noticed the bottle of tequila still on the counter top and grabbed it to pour myself another shot. I scratched my head, wondering where this display of emotion was coming from. After all, he had cancelled out on me a few short hours earlier. He didn't have the common decency to speak to me; he had left the message on the fucking answering machine. He stood there looking at me, waiting for my response. I waited briefly to gather my thoughts, before I decided to answer his questions.

"Who the fuck do you think you are, coming into my house this time of night with this bullshit? For the record, your punk ass called me when you knew I was on my way home from work to meet you; leaving me a half-assed message about changing your plans. Now I'm not stupid, Kevin. I knew when I played that message that you were either growing tired of spending time with me, or you had made other plans." I found my voice rising as I continued to read him the riot act.

"You think I didn't know you were probably going to be out looking around for some ass? How fucking stupid do you think I am? I know you been spending time with me, and you aren't getting anything here. So all this while, I am sure you wanted to get your rocks off. But the fucked-up part about it, Kevin, is that you didn't think I shared those same feelings. Yes, as much as you wanted to fuck, I wanted to get fucked, but you couldn't bring yourself to think about fucking me because I was positive." The can of worms had been opened and there was no going back.

"You thought you were doing me a fucking favor by hanging out with me? You thought, oh well, let me be nice to him because he's positive and I know how lonely it can be for someone like him. Baby, trust, I am not yours or anybody else's charity case. If I want to get fucked or get my dick sucked, or even have someone just spend time with me, that is not the issue. I thought by being myself around you, that you would see me for more than being positive. But you can't seem to get past that, so you should get the fuck out of my house and my life."

The slap isn't as good when you are on the receiving end of it. I could tell my words struck him as his did me. But I wasn't finished. The years of hurt and frustration came out at this moment. It didn't matter who the recipient was of this verbal ass whipping; Kevin just happened to get it as it came.

"You think I wanted that brother up on my ass tonight? No! I wanted to be with you and I held back. I didn't want to scare you off or put you in a position to make you feel uncomfortable. All the while my feelings are growing for you each and every day. After being told I was going to die twenty years ago, spending the better part of that time hoping that I would find someone to love me wasn't easy, by any means. I spent this time with you praying for time, asking God to see me through whatever He had planned for me with you. And here you are, pitying me, scared to even fucking touch me."

With that last line, I felt my lips tremble. I had cried once in front of him and with the alcohol serving as the conduit for my words and actions, I began to feel myself doing it again.

"You see, you don't have to deal with or pity me. I do that enough on my own. You wanted ass tonight, so instead of coming here to make me feel bad about doing what I did tonight, you could be with that little bitch you were up on this evening."

The thought of him being with someone else at this moment made me cry, even though we were engaged in this heated exchange.

I stopped for a moment, looking away from him. By this time, the tequila was fucking with me and made me bold enough to take the next step.

"If you want a piece of ass, here, take it."

I ripped the shirt that covered my body, buttons flying and landing at his feet. I kicked off the boots and found myself losing all dignity as I removed the jeans and boxers, finally exposing my naked body in front of him. At this point, I had no shame.

"You want some ass?" I stepped closer to him, fumbling at his belt buckle with force, waiting for some reaction from him. "Come on, Kevin, be a man. Fuck me!" I continued the chant, loosening his belt buckle.

He grabbed my hands, pushing me away. This behavior was not in my thoughts as I had lain in bed many nights, thinking of being with him. I felt his hands push me away, and I caught myself before I could fall to the floor.

With my back toward him, standing completely naked, tears streaming down my face, I yelled one last time, "Get the fuck out!"

I heard no movement coming from his direction. My focus was now on, not only picking up my clothes, but picking up my face. I leaned against the table, wiping my eyes, wishing that he would leave. Now I knew I could never face him again.

I heard the boots as they got closer to me. I turned around, attempting to make my way to the door to assist him in leaving. He blocked my route as he grabbed me in his arms.

"Please, Kevin, get off of me. Get out!"

As much as I fought to get away from his embrace, he held me tighter. I started to cry uncontrollably. I buried my face deep in his chest, my shirt slipping off my shoulder. I felt the moisture from his face as he held me. I was exhausted and collapsed into his arms. No other words were spoken or needed to be spoken at that moment. We both cried in each other's arms, hoping our words had not destroyed what we both wanted from each other—love.

KEVIN

I couldn't sleep after our huge blow-up on the previous night. I was able to make my way around Mark's kitchen, searching out the necessities to create a makeshift breakfast and coffee. I figured when he finally arose, he would have a hangover. I had the coffee brewing; hoping the scent of the fresh pot would stir him from his sleep. I had picked up the clothes that were stripped by him from the argument and had placed them neatly on the loveseat. I sat at the table, attempting to finish the script to the stage play that had unfolded only a few hours earlier. I wanted to make sure he was alright before I made my exit stage left. I could have easily abandoned him at that moment, but I wanted to see how the play ended. In my heart, I wanted to end on a good note. I wanted the storyline to play out the way I saw in old movies, but because of our exchange and the intensity of the words, I truly didn't believe it to be in the cards. As the coffee in my mug became a little warm to the taste, I refilled it to take the edge off of the few beers I had plowed my body with.

Why did it have to go there? I wish I could have been man enough to express what I was feeling to Mark without having the situation escalate. I saw in his face and eyes, and heard through his words, years of pent-up hostility, anger and sadness. I was yet another man in a long line to break his heart. I rehearsed what I would say in my thoughts. After holding him, I wanted to be with him. It was pretty fucked up that I had allowed it to go as far as it did. It was also fucked up that I couldn't tell him what I was feeling as he so eloquently told me. Mind you, he was drunk when he did it, but nevertheless, his words hit close to home.

As I walked around the downstairs, I felt a certain calm after the storm. I felt like I was home in this place that was foreign to me. I noticed how meticulous he was with every photo in place, perfectly angled to highlight the journey of his life. I saw pictures of those I presumed were family and friends. Some photos led me to believe he saved pictures of past loves by the display of silent affection.

I sat on the sofa imagining what life would be like with him. I imagined what it would be like to come home to him and see photos of the two of us placed strategically around our place. I saw the two of us rousing from sleep to have coffee together, discussing our plans for the day. During all of this foreshadowing, the thing that stuck out the most, was just sharing this walk with him.

MARK

My head was pounding when I woke up. I could still taste the tequila in my mouth from last night and the effects it had left from doing too much. Over the years, I had learned how to drink in moderation, but the events of the evening had led me to believe I could handle it. Boy, was I mistaken. My bed felt good because it was the one place I truly felt safe from the outside world. I could tell something was different because I could feel the sheets against my skin. I wasn't one for sleeping in the nude, even in the sanctity of my own bed, but as I pulled the covers back, I noticed I was naked. The memories of the night were vague to me. I remembered hanging out and drinking too much, but after crying, I had lost all track of what had happened. How did I end up this way? I don't know why I did what I did next, but I ran my fingers between my ass cheeks to see if anything seemed out of place. There were times in my youth, when I'd had too much to drink, and awoke to the feel of Vaseline or some type of lube between my legs from getting fucked. I hoped that this wasn't the case this morning. Had I allowed myself to have sex without protection? Since testing positive, I made sure that everyone I was with used a condom when penetrating me, for fear of transmitting the virus to anyone. I felt a sense of relief when I felt my asshole was dry and still intact.

I lay in bed for a few more minutes, trying to deal with the throbbing of my temples. I massaged both sides, hoping it would offer some relief. I avoided looking out the window since the sun was shining brightly through the half-closed blinds. Of all days, I wished it had rained to match the mood I was in. I only wanted to stay in bed and avoid the world after last night. I tried to remember exactly what had happened that had led to this hangover. With my eyes closed, I remembered everything. I saw myself showing out at the Mill, and even remembered vividly the heated exchange I'd had with Kevin. I realized, at that moment, one of the reasons I didn't drink tequila as much. It made me into a raving bitch. It provided me with the courage to say what I wanted to say, no matter how the message was delivered. At that moment, I figured out how I had ended up naked. I had ruined a perfectly good shirt by ripping it and stripping myself, not only of my clothing, but what was left of my dignity. My headache became worse at the thought of my actions and needed immediate relief.

I managed to get my ass out of bed and headed toward the bathroom. I ran the water and checked its temperature before getting in. I grabbed a couple of aspirin from the medicine cabinet and drank the water from the shower to wash them down. I felt my hair lay down immediately as I pushed my head under the showerhead for added relief.

I stayed in the shower until it turned cold enough for me to tolerate. I felt a little better, but needed to kill the taste of the lingering tequila in my mouth. I opted to gargle rather than brush my teeth. I would be heading downstairs for a cup of coffee in a matter of minutes, and I didn't like the combined taste of toothpaste and coffee. I rinsed for a few minutes, before grabbing my robe to warm myself.

I heard noises coming from the kitchen as I descended the stairs. I became frightened by what would greet me. The last thing I remembered, or could recollect, was the arguing and crying I had done when Kevin was here. I tiptoed quietly so not to disturb what was going on. I prayed that I hadn't left the door open and someone hadn't decided to enter and take what valuables I had left. This was one on those times I wished I had a gun, or something to protect me from what I was about to face.

When I peeked around the banister, I saw Kevin standing there, wearing only his jeans. I breathed a sigh of relief, but wasn't quite sure what I was about to face, coming from him.

I was at a loss for words when I saw him. His body was even better than I imagined. I enjoyed the sight of him for a brief moment, unsure of what to say as I headed toward the cupboard to grab a cup. As I got closer to the coffeemaker, Kevin moved away to take a seat at the table. I noticed he had poured me a cup of coffee, after hearing the shower running earlier. We were both silent as I grabbed the cream and sweetener. I had my back toward him, trying to think of something to say, unsure of what my drunken thoughts and behavior had revealed last night.

I turned toward him, admiring the definition of his body. Damn, this man was fine. It would have made the moment so much easier and less tense if we had not had the blow-up. But it happened, and there was no way to turn back the hands of time. Believe me, if anyone knew you couldn't go back to change the outcome of one's behavior, it was me. There were nights I stared at the ceiling, wishing I could return to the first time I didn't use a condom. I think back at that night, although pleasurable and satisfying; I realize that it was the night that changed my life forever. If I could wave a wand over the last twenty years, maybe I wouldn't be at this moment searching for the right words.

I knew the conversation was coming and I couldn't avoid it. I just didn't know how it was coming, so I prepared myself. For the first time in a long time, I had to take responsibility for my actions and the words I had allowed to freely come out of my mouth. I had to be a man and face what was to come next. I quietly took a seat across from Kevin at the table to hear my punishment.

KEVIN

Even fucked up with a hangover, he was a sight to behold. This was the first time I was able to see the natural beauty of his face. His eyes were bloodshot from the combined drinking and crying. I knew the alcohol aided with the attitude, but it was me, the bearer of the tears. I felt guilt creep in, and as I asked how he was doing, his face answered my question, with a look of sadness and regret. After some bad shit in the past, with guys who showed their asses while intoxicated over stupid shit, I avoided them. But here I was, fighting the reality that had built up over this time I spent with Mark. For every reason I found not to be with him, mainly because he was positive, my heart told me that this was the one for me. We looked at each other, trying to apologize to the other with silence. Our eyes said everything our mouths couldn't say. We sat there continuing to sip our coffee without a word. It was tense, to say the least, but I needed to break the silence.

"I'm sorry."

I hung my head in shame for hurting him; that was not my intent. When I found the nerve to look at him, I hoped my apologies were enough to take back last evening. When I saw that it opened the door slightly for his forgiveness, I decided to push my way in even further. I finally had to fess up and tell him what was on my mind.

"You don't know how fucked up I am right now. I see in you everything I want, man. I see this good-looking man across from me, and yet he scares the shit out of me." I could tell by his puzzled look, he didn't know where I was going. "I see every-thing in you that I thought about having in a relationship. You are smart, and you have a kind heart. And as much as I have tried to distance myself from the fact that you have HIV, I have to admit, it bothers the shit out of me. On one hand, I feel bad; really I do. I want to fuck up the motherfucker who did this to you. But then I find myself angry with you. I think, how could you let someone do that? With all the shit that was out there about this shit, how could you play Russian Roulette with your life?" I could see my attempts to apologize weren't doing what I hoped they would.

"Mark, as much as the fear of being with you scares the fuck out of me, the thought of you not being in my life at this moment, fucks me up even more."

There, I finally said it. It didn't come out all romantic and shit, but I finally said what had been bothering me for the longest time. I looked away from him; the bitch in me was about to creep in. I wanted this man in my life. I needed him to teach me about his joys and sorrows. I needed him to educate me on how to love him and make love to him. I needed him to stay alive for me to love and be loved by him. I needed him to live, so that we may live and love together for what time we had left. No one is ever promised tomorrow, but if it was a written guarantee, I wanted to share it with him. I swallowed my pride and got up from the chair. I walked toward Mark, kneeling at his feet, eventually finding a spot on the floor in front of him.

I buried my face in his robe and begged him, "Don't die on me, baby. I love you."

MARK

At the moment I heard his declaration of his love for me, I was reminded of a question a friend once asked me: "When was the last time someone told you they loved you and you actually felt it?" I couldn't give an honest answer. It had been awhile since anyone, outside of family and friends, had said those three words to me. I wanted to interrupt this moment between Kevin and me to run to the telephone to call the friend and share with him the answer. This was the first time I heard the words. The first time they penetrated so deeply. The first time they meant something. This wasn't about saying those words to get something in return. This time it warmed me. It made me feel something I had buried deep inside. It made me feel the same way.

I didn't want to say something that I would regret later as I had done the previous night. I raised Kevin's face to greet mine and smiled through the hangover. I stood, grabbing his hand in mine and guiding him toward the stairs. He allowed me to lead the way as we entered my bedroom. I closed the blinds, eliminating the sunlight, and removed my robe. I stood there nervous and scared. I remembered how last night I had exposed myself in a fit of rage, but here, I stood completely vulnerable. I was not one of the worked-out muscle queens who ventured to the gym on a regular basis to tease those they sought to bed. I attempted to cover certain parts of my body because I felt inadequate in certain areas. I was careful not to turn around with my back toward him to see that I lacked the round, full ass of the brother I had seen him dancing with. But I hoped that it would be sufficient enough to enjoy what it was capable of doing. I watched him as he came closer to me. For a brief moment, I wanted to turn away because of uncertainty, but I wanted him. He gently cupped my chin, raising my face toward his and softly kissing my lips. I tasted the remains of the coffee on his lips, as his tongue extended gently into my mouth, parting my lips. I closed my eyes as he tenderly explored my mouth with his tongue. The feelings of inadequacy left as I reached my arms around his neck and returned his kiss. It was not a kiss of rushing through a meal to get to dessert. It was the beginning of the meal.

I felt Kevin wrap his arms around my waist and grab me closer into him. I had dreamed many a night for this moment and it was actually happening. I returned the passion of his kiss and taste, as he held me closer. His hands slid down my torso, making me flinch at his exploration. I continued to kiss him, never wanting the kiss to end. I got lost in the tenderness of his lips, only to have him gently push me away. With my eyes still closed, I blindly searched for this missing part. Eventually, I opened my eyes to see him looking at me. Fearing the worst, I backed away. He smiled assuredly that everything was okay.

Picking up where we had left off, I felt Kevin's hands exploring my body. With each touch, my dick got harder. The reality of this kiss surpassed any of my dreams of this moment. His hands traveled from the nape of my neck to the small of my back, sending tingles up and down my spine. I shivered from his touch. He had me at an unfair advantage; he was still clothed from the waist down. When I felt his hands rest right above my ass, the jeans that possessed what I had longed for since meeting him, his manhood, jumped a little against my leg.

I guided Kevin to the bed, allowing myself to sit on the edge with him standing before me. It was unfair for me to be naked alone. I took my hand and traced the bulge in his pants ever so gently. As I ran my fingers across the shaft, it continued to grow slowly. Even though we were in semi-darkness, I noticed the outline of his dick. I raised my head a bit to taste the sprout of hair rising from the waistband of the jeans he wore. It was salty from dancing the night before, but still possessed the scent of the body wash he used before going out, I presumed. I allowed my tongue to separate the strands as I enjoyed circling my tongue around each one.

I rested my head on his torso for a moment, as his fingers ran through my hair. His touch felt good. I inhaled him, taking in the complementary scents as I contemplated my next move. I lowered my face to his crotch, softly rubbing my face against his semi-hard dick. I pleaded silently with him for more as I looked up at him. I searched for permission on his face, as I loosened the belt buckle and the button that separated him from my mouth. I never liked the taste of latex in my mouth when giving head to anyone. I allowed them to decide if it was something they wanted to use to protect themselves. This time, I took it upon myself to reach for the flavored condoms in the nightstand to cover Kevin before I allowed him into my mouth. We both knew what was safe and unsafe. In a perfect world, I would have been able to swallow him without the condom, but I wanted to give him the right to make that decision.

He stepped back for a moment as I reached for the condom. If Kevin was like others from my past, he didn't enjoy being blown with the rubber on. For a moment, I figured it would be a deal breaker. I wanted to taste him in all of his natural splendor. I searched for a flavor that was as close to the taste it pretended to be. The flavors left very little to be desired, but I wanted to protect him. While I fumbled through the nightstand, he must have made the decision on his own. When I began to open the package, he grabbed my hand to say no. I looked up and asked if he was sure and he nodded silently. I asked once again before I proceeded, and again I was met with disapproval.

I placed the condom on the nightstand and resumed where I had left off. I quickly unbuttoned his jeans and noticed Kevin wasn't wearing underwear. I placed my hands inside to push his dick aside as I unzipped his pants, avoiding catching his pubic hair in the chain. I lowered his pants enough to see how thick and long he was. As I continued to lower them, there was more of him to see. Finally, with his jeans now at his ankles, he stepped out of them, exposing all of himself to me. I had been with brothers before with big dicks, but for a brief moment, Kevin scared me. I wasn't sure if I was going to be able to handle him. I was used to getting drunk or high to have sex. I felt, at the time, that I was fortunate to have someone to be intimate with me, regardless of how the person looked or treated me. I would find myself at the bottom of a bottle in order to go through with the fucking or sucking granted to me. The alcohol and drugs numbed the pain in so many ways. Here and now, outside of a slight hangover from the past evening, I found myself sober and unsure. I was so intimidated by the length and girth of his dick that I honestly thought about excusing myself to take a couple of shots of tequila. I decided against this. I wanted to experience, for once, the pain and the pleasure of having my wits about me.

During the brief flashback in my thoughts, Kevin's erection

started to slowly go away. As I stared at it, it began to sloop downward facing me; even semi-hard, it was threatening. I lowered my mouth to the head, wrapping my lips around it. With my mouth, I was able to bring it up with my lips firmly wrapped around the head. I could feel the weight of it, as I forced it back to attention. I opened my mouth as wide as I could, taking more of him into my mouth. Like the bad porn movies of the 1970s, with each inch of him entering my mouth, I raised my eyes to see if my performance met his approval. He returned my gaze for a moment as I sucked him deeper, forgoing any discomfort to please him. When he tilted his head back, I knew I was doing something right.

With each swab of the bottom of the shaft with my tongue, he continued to grow. I felt my mouth widen, as he grabbed the back of my head, slowly grinding as much in as he could. The shaft seemed to be thicker at the base as I slid down, wanting to please him. At times, I felt myself about to choke, and after feeling the gag reflex in the back of my throat, he slowed down. I was able to catch my breath before I continued. I could smell the sweat from his pubes as he pushed me down deeper on him. I allowed the back of my throat to relax more, gently swallowing and tightening my throat around the head of his dick. I pulled back to catch a second breath and tasted his sweet pre-cum. That was more of an incentive to continue. I sucked him back in, hitting the back of my throat and allowing myself to swallow more of his nut. He pulled out, fearing he was going to cum too soon, and guided my shoulders toward the mattress.

Before he joined me, he positioned me so that I was no longer on the edge of the bed, but rightfully in the middle, with my head propped on the pillows. He allowed his muscular body to lie on me without discomfort to me. With one hand wrapped around my neck to bring me closer to him, he parted my legs with his, resting between mine.

I felt the combination of saliva and pre-cum from his dick resting on my stomach as he drove his tongue into my mouth. He started slowly grinding into me as his mouth now made its way to my neck. With one long lick, I next felt his tongue darting in and out of my ear. I returned his movement, by matching his with the same intensity. He raised himself a bit and positioned his dick between my legs. I wanted to feel him inside of me as he continued to grind. He continued working on my neck and ear, switching up to see which area brought more joy and reaction. His full lips found that one spot on my neck and sucked it as a reward for giving him head. I stretched my neck to allow him more room to play as he continued grinding into me.

I reached my arms around him, only to have him remove them and pin me down gently. I raised my legs ever so slightly to allow him deeper between my thighs. On occasion, he would force himself up by holding me down to look at me. I didn't want him to stop.

In between the kissing and the friction his dick created between my legs, I felt the head right at the entrance of my hole. I wanted to feel him inside of me, nothing between us but the air we shared, but I knew that was not possible. With each thrust, I felt him slowly entering me. I pleaded with him to stop, but he was determined.

I fought not only with myself, and the thoughts of fucking without a condom, but also the force with which he held me down. I wanted him, but not at the risk of infecting him. I raised my legs more, which allowed me positioning to place them around his waist. With all of my might, I tightened my thighs, signaling him to stop and prevent any further intrusion.

He took note of what was happening and found his way back in the moment. He relaxed the tension on my arms and sat up. He looked away as he realized what had almost happened. We waited for a moment, both realizing what could have turned out to be a bad situation. In that short time, Kevin started to get out of the bed, reaching for his pants. I stopped him. I grabbed him to come back to bed; he returned with some reservations.

As he lay there, I noticed he became soft again. He apologized for what had happened and I informed him it was okay. He motioned to leave again, but I stopped him. If this were to happen again, as I hoped it would, I had to show him.

With him lying there on his back, I started once again by blowing him. This was the taste that would nourish me for some time to come. In this position, I was able to control how much I took in. His drive had returned as I felt him growing in my mouth once again. When he was fully erect, I straddled his stomach. Leaning over, I reached for the condom and lube in the nightstand to educate Kevin.

I placed the lube in my hands to warm it before I massaged his dick. It took more than usual, but I made sure that all areas of him were covered. I removed the condom from the covering, being extra careful not to break it or tear it. With Kevin's dick in my hand, I rolled the condom over the head. It was a good thing I added enough lube; for a moment, it looked like it would not fit. I gently rolled it down with both hands, applying additional lube to it. With the rubber neatly and securely in place, I applied another light coating to his dick, especially the head. I knew this is where I would have the most trouble.

After I prepared him, I went about taking care of myself. I applied as much to my ass as I did to the condom and Kevin's dick. I raised myself on my feet, still straddling Kevin and held him in my hands as I lowered myself on him. I closed my eyes and bit my lip.

I sat atop him for minutes, as I worked the head of his dick into me. With what seemed to be less than half of the head in, I removed it. There was a sharp, piercing pain that I couldn't describe, but I realized where it came from. I repositioned myself again and restarted.

I felt my ass slowly open as Kevin lay patiently for me to adjust. I slowly lowered myself, flinching in pain. He placed his hands around my ass cheeks to help spread them, as my hand continued to control how much I allowed of him inside me. I could feel my muscles tighten around him as I continued to lower myself on him. He continued to help as I leaned forward to kiss him once again. Feeling his tongue in my mouth relaxed me more, allowing him to fully enjoy me.

He waited for me to signal to him to continue. I almost wanted to give up and save this for a later time, but I endured. He eased the pain I was experiencing by continuing to take my mind off of it with his kisses. With each taste of his tongue, I found myself turned on more and more. I was able to slowly rise up and down, returning to my original position with him completely inside me. For the first few moments, each time his dick was exposed to air, I applied more lube for comfort for the two of us. I eventually found a happy medium between pleasure and pain, as I rose about him. In and out.

Time had passed and pain eventually made way for pleasure. The slow strides I made in riding Kevin were now replaced with my own form of teasing him. The passion I felt for him, and the unspoken love contained in my heart for him, forced me to show him what I couldn't say. I squeezed the shaft of his dick tightly to remind him where he was. With each squeeze, he released a moan and a grunt. He returned the favor, by expanding my hole more with quick, pulsating thrusts, to remind me where I was.

I continued to ride Kevin, feeling him long dick me from this position. He leaned forward, sitting upright, wrapping his arms around my body. I dug my feet into the bed, as his embrace kept me stationary for his pleasure. I eventually wrapped my legs around his waist, holding on as he dug deeper into me. I started to cry as he fucked me. I wriggled to get more and more of him in me. We paused for a moment, taking a break to kiss and stare into each other's eyes.

With his arms wrapped around me, and his dick securely stuck in my hole, he inched his way down to the edge of the bed. Still seated on him, he rocked back and forth, going deeper than anyone who had been there before him. I was losing my fucking mind.

What came next was a scene only reserved for fantasies or done by heterosexuals. Kevin placed his arms beneath my legs while seated. He positioned them over his shoulders, as he raised up, holding me tightly. Recognizing my discomfort from this position, he walked slowly to the wall, resting my back against it. With skillful precision, he fucked me against the wall, preventing any idea or room for escape. I couldn't move as he continued taking advantage of the situation. We remained for a few moments until his legs began to wobble.

I was caught up in the moment, as he lay me on my back. I needed to check before we went any further; if the condom was intact. I asked Kevin to stop briefly so I could slowly ease him out of me. After careful inspection, everything was alright.

I decided, during this brief break, to replace the condom with another for our next round. It didn't take too long before Kevin brought me to the edge of the bed and grabbed my ankles to rest on his shoulder. My ass appeared to have reverted to its normal size after the initial pounding, but he masterfully entered me once again.

He took his time as he held my legs apart. I noticed as he watched his dick disappear in and out. He would look up at me to see if I were okay. This time, he grabbed the lube, squeezing more onto the shaft of his dick as he pushed deeper into me. I wanted to cum as I felt him tease my hole.

As he continued plowing my ass, I reached for the lube and took matters in my own hand. I needed to cum. Each time he pulled out to the head, he would wait a moment, feeling me tightening before he pushed in again. My ass puckered, causing my legs to tremble as he held me by the ankles. I started working on my dick with the same precision he used on my hole. I pushed back because it felt good. I started to thrash around as Kevin plunged deeper. I couldn't hold back. With each thrust, I found myself closer to cumming. He knew it, he felt it, and he increased his speed. I slid down more so that he could have more. I started working my dick into a frenzy. With one quick arch of my back, meeting the last deep-dicked thrust of his, we both came. Our voices carried throughout the house. His "Oh God," and my loud sighs and moans of pleasure, echoed. He lowered my ankles, my legs still trembling, and fell on me. I wrapped my arms around his waist, our sweat combined. And without cue or cause, at the same time, we whispered, what we both knew and finally felt, "I love you."

KEVIN

If I were a smoker, I would have reached for a cigarette after making love with Mark. Our bodies were drained from this exchange of passion. After taking a quick shower, we crawled back into bed and fell asleep. The pillow that I held earlier on in this vision of him was now replaced with the real thing. Like hibernating bears, he snuggled close to me, finding the perfect place to nestle. I held on tight as his backside rested against my chest. I was happy we were able to get beyond the games we had played with each other the previous night. We were both too old to get involved in that sissy shit. As much as I fought to keep my eyes open and watch him sleep, hearing the silent whimpers he made while asleep, I eventually dozed off with a smile on my face.

We lost the remainder of the day as we slept. When we eventually awoke, dusk had replaced the sunshine from the early morning. We retreated downstairs to find something to eat to replenish the energy we had spent making love. I wasn't too much of a cook, usually settled for take-out or cereal, but I watched as Mark went about the kitchen humming to make a meal out of the cupboard's contents. He signaled me to grab the plates, as I inhaled the wafting aroma in the air. With a few shakes of some seasoning and a quick turn on the stove, we sat down to sage chicken breasts and steamed vegetables. I wasn't used to eating healthy shit like this. As far as chicken was concerned, it was fried and smothered with hot sauce, but I tried it. The tastes were different, but they certainly complemented one another. I ate heartily as we sat and made small talk. There were some things I wanted to address before the evening was over, like whether I was going to receive an invitation to spend the night. We continued to eat until I realized, looking at my plate, everything was gone. Mark removed the plates and placed them in his dishwasher and then he went about cleaning the mess he had made. I walked into the living room and searched for a happy distraction until he had finished. I wound up adjusting the radio dial for something quiet and soothing.

I came across what seemed to be old-time jazz or standards. The singer faintly sounded like Frank Sinatra and that was good enough for me. It wasn't my thing, but it was good for the moment.

I settled in on the sofa, sinking into it after the workout, still tired and waiting to return to bed. Mark offered a glass of wine from the kitchen and I accepted. When he finally made his way to me in the living room, I sat up to make room for him next to me.

We listened to the noise from outside the thin walls that confined us as it fought for our attention with the radio. We both sipped our wine, waiting for the other to break the silence.

I finally took the lead and broke the silence. I thought back for a moment to making love to him and how I had enjoyed it. I didn't think much of it at the time, when he was sucking my dick, the risks associated with HIV. I guess all the blood had rushed to the wrong head, and now I found myself questioning whether it was safe for me. I decided to choose my words carefully because I didn't want him to feel badly. Hell, it was my decision not to use the condom while he sucked my dick. But now, in hindsight, I wanted a little more information. I guess, I needed him to tell me it was okay.

He placed the glass on the table and searched for the answers in his head. He explained that HIV was transmitted sometimes during oral sex, if blood was present and there were open cuts, even around my piss hole, that could transmit the virus. He reminded me that he didn't brush his teeth before going down on me, and his oral hygiene was something he prided himself on. I sensed he felt uncomfortable having this conversation as the look on his face changed. I broke the tension with my attempt at humor by telling him his oral hygiene wasn't the only oral skill he should be proud about. That seemed to make him laugh, and I decided to quickly change the conversation. I can't lie, I had enjoyed it. And any other time I wouldn't have questioned a brother sucking my dick, however, the fact that he was positive did bother me. But I had to be responsible for my actions.

We sat there continuing to listen to the music. I presumed it was his favorite radio station as he hummed along with the songs in between our conversation. I searched his face for his thoughts, unsure of what to say or do next.

I grabbed him and pulled him closer to me. He rested his head safely on my shoulder, answering any and all questions that were unspoken. I didn't have to ask for permission to spend the night; it was a given. I didn't have to ask, nor did we have to discuss what would come next—we both knew. I was home now, and I wasn't going anywhere.

MARK

I t wasn't much longer after that beautiful Saturday morning that Kevin moved in with me. Since my place was bigger, we agreed that we would stay here until we found a place we both liked; one we could both call our own. In the past, there were brothers we had both moved in with early on in relationships; only to have them show their asses and play that trump card of it was "their" place. He was a little reluctant, at first, but we both agreed it was temporary. After work, we found ourselves covering the D.C. area, even considering locations in Northern Virginia that we would call ours. Some places were much too small for the area's prices. Some didn't provide the amenities that we both wanted: a washer and dryer; a spare room in case one got pissed with the other and wanted to take a break. Come on, we were realists.

As much as our love was growing, there were things we both did that got on each other's nerves. My pet peeve with Kevin was his leaving dishes in the sink, rather than taking the extra minute or two to rinse them before placing them in the dishwasher. He was bothered by how much of a clean freak I was. I had a Saturday ritual that I stuck by, even after he moved in. I would faithfully get up, put on some music and go about cleaning. At times, you could literally eat off the floor. He enjoyed lying in bed on Saturday mornings, eating cereal and flipping channels. As much as I enjoyed lying in bed with him on the weekends, knowing we didn't have to rush about to get ready for work, I had shit to do.

I would sometimes start in the bedroom. Kevin had a tendency to step out of his clothes and leave them on the floor for me to pick up. We had our defined roles in the relationship, but it never allowed either of us to question that we were both men. He liked to do what he liked to do, including fixing gadgets around the house that I would never take the time to entertain. He could sit at the kitchen table or sit up in bed tinkering with some shit, making a mess, and there I was to clean it up.

I took pride in cleaning the place so that if we invited friends or family over, it didn't require much tidying. We both took turns cooking, even if at times his meals left little to be desired. I have to give him credit for trying. There was love in each meal he prepared. Sometimes we got a bit out of pocket with each other when we were a little pissed. We certainly didn't spare feelings with some of the shit we said to each other, but we knew there were invisible lines not to cross. We sometimes got pretty close, but never crossed them.

"Why don't you pick up your nasty-ass drawers, Kevin?" would come out of my mouth as I went about cleaning, leaving behind his response. Downstairs, I grabbed the cleaning supplies from underneath the sink, dusting and spraying, vacuuming, only to feel him catch me off guard by standing behind me; him being naked. He knew how to make me forget about the anger with one simple hug.

We finally narrowed our search to a place we both liked. I didn't want to give up the place on the Hill because it was convenient to work, but we both had agreed to find our place together. We stayed on the Hill. It was a few blocks further from what I was used to walking to get to work daily, but close enough to access the Metro. It was a beautiful, three-bedroom near Union Station. Of course, we decided on the master bedroom and what color scheme would be suitable for the two of us. The medium-sized room would be reserved for visitors, and it was great that it was at the opposite end of the hallway. The smaller of the three served as a catch-all storage area. When we moved in, we sometimes agreed to disagree on where to place certain items, or what to keep or discard. There were little things that were special to both of us, but being in the relationship, we compromised on what to let go. Sometimes I found him sneaking back to the boxes of stuff we had agreed to donate to remove an item to store deep in the closet. I never let on that I knew what he was doing. Behind his back, I had retrieved a couple of my own discarded treasures.

We were now in our place, making our memories. It was something I thought could never happen. Our lovemaking was still as beautiful as it was the very first time. One thing that we learned to do, that became vital in our relationship, was to communicate with each other. If at times, he felt uncomfortable with our sexual play, we didn't have a problem stopping in the moment to discuss it. We found if we discussed it openly and continued with no hard feelings, it intensified the moment. We found ourselves at times reading online information and available reading materials on HIV/AIDS to make sure that we were not only safe, but aware of anything new that could alter this beautiful reality.

I remember the first HIV test Kevin had after our first sexual encounter. He was nervous as shit. I volunteered to go with him, since I knew what it was like for me to go alone. As he disappeared behind the closed door, I silently prayed that everything was okay. I know it was ultimately his decision not to wear a condom when I went down on him, and I hoped this test wouldn't change his life. He spent a great deal of time in the office, and I could only imagine him informing the tester of his act of transgression with me. Whatever the discussion, I wasn't privy to it as he came out to greet me. We walked silently to the car and continued to observe this moment of quiet time until we got home. I didn't want to push the issue and ask what he was thinking. I allowed him to shut down until he was ready to talk about it. He shared his concerns, but not to alarm me or make me feel bad. I reminded him, that no matter what, I was there with him; that seemed to calm him. We spent the next week or so waiting for the results, and we both exhaled a sigh of relief when they came back negative. When that was said and done, that's when we decided to make sure we talked about anything and everything we did sexually. What was safe for the two of us. And let me tell you, after discussing such matters for the first time in my life with a partner, a boyfriend, or anyone for that matter, the sex was the shit.

I was satisfied with Kevin. I had boyfriends in the past who cheated on me, even fucked friends of mine, figuring I would never hear about it. But that was something I frowned upon. Kevin and I would lay up at night until the wee hours of the morning, talking about infidelity and how it hurt like a bitch. We were both equally attractive, but he possessed an air of cocky arrogance that attracted others to him. I was sometimes jealous when I would excuse myself to go to the bathroom at a club or bar on the nights we did venture out. As with vultures on the prey, those queens would flock to Kevin like stink on shit before I could step four feet away. Upon returning, I could see them hanging on to his every word as they sized him up. Seeing that

I was approaching, Kevin would point in my direction. Some-times over the loud music, I could hear him say, "You see him? That's me." I would walk up and he would place his arms around my waist, sensing that I was pissed.

He laughed it off at times, but he knew it bothered me. He was always telling me I had nothing to worry about. He was getting everything he needed at home. On the rare occasion, I blew that shit off, I would remind him, "If you feel the need to fuck someone else, don't come back." With that warning, Kevin never cheated on me.

After completing the chores I assigned myself on Saturday mornings, we would hop in Kevin's car, searching for shit to add to our new home. At times, we decided together; at times, we disagreed. We started to act like an old married couple. We had a group of true friends we spent time with on weekends. Although we ventured to the Mill to get our dance on, our weekends were usually spent hosting a movie-theme night or playing board games and cards. I loved my baby with all of my heart, but he could certainly renege playing Spades. It got to the point I didn't like partnering with him; I enjoyed winning. But we never allowed our talking shit to go any further than the table.

Movie nights were fun. We would pick a film genre out of a hat and spend separate times at the video store finding some-thing that fell within that genre. We wouldn't allow the other to know the film title until it was placed in the VCR. If it was just the two of us, we would adjourn to the bedroom to stretch out with the snacks we had purchased and cuddle. Sometimes we had to pause the film, depending on how late it was, for me to take my meds. When I returned to bed, I would find my rightful place in his arms again, as he loved playing with my hair and falling asleep.

Outside of the constant side effects of my medications, life was good. I was taking better care of myself, learning how to eat healthier and to alleviate the stress in my life. My friends and family saw the joy in my face and heard it in my voice when we spoke or visited. If someone had told me years ago that I would be in love, I would have thought they were pulling my leg, or feeding me some bullshit to make me happy. At the time, "happiness" and "love" were two words that didn't go together, or even come close in my vocabulary. I had a death sentence, and I figured that whatever time I had left, I would spend it alone. But my friends and family were all right about my current joy. Here I was in love with someone, who in return, was in love with me. On the nights I fell asleep either on his chest or in his arms, it reminded me of my dreams of loving someone and the reality of those dreams coming true. I didn't want anyone to think that Kevin's love was the shot I needed to take care of myself from that moment on; I was doing a pretty good job of it before him. But it was his love, his growing love, his daily love, that convinced me to do everything in my power to make the time that we had together something that both he and I could treasure. It would be this love that would carry him through some of the most difficult times that we would face in the future. But, for now, I loved being in love.

KEVIN

My buddies joked with me when they came over to convince me to head out with them to the clubs. They would say shit like, "So are you the mommy or the daddy?"

Sucking my teeth and giving it back to them, I would respond, "Really depends on the mood I'm in. Don't hate, bitch."

My life, with Mark in it, had changed for the better. If he wasn't in the picture, I would have been eager to hit the streets and the bars. But each time I went out with them, I was reminded of what I really wanted. For some of these brothers I saw, this was their only existence—being the loud-mouthed center of attention; disguising the emptiness and loneliness they felt. I often watched them hit on brothers they knew were out of their league. They were boisterous, sometimes obnoxious, touching people on their asses or grabbing their dicks just for touch or reaction from someone. Naw, man, that shit wasn't for me.

Mark didn't much care for the bar scene. I was surprised, with him being a smoker and all, that he found it difficult to bear the smell of cigarettes in a smoky environment. That was one of the major issues with us moving in together. I didn't smoke, but I tolerated his smoking because of my love for him. We agreed that with this new place we called home that he would not smoke in the house. His smoking was reserved to the back porch of the house where I set up a small table and chair for him. He was respectful of this wish of mine, and he never came to bed smelling like an ashtray. My baby was fresh every night; if he wasn't, he would not be laying up on me.

Now, don't get me wrong. It may sound like Mark and I were up under each other twenty-four/seven, but we weren't. He had his moments of hanging out with his friends as much as I did. I didn't trust some of those bitches when I first met them. There were times when Mark would show his jealousy when someone approached me while we were out. But I knew where my heart was. And the same can be said for him. There were motherfuckers who tried me when we were out, pushing up on him and saying off-the-wall shit. There were a couple of times I was ready to fuck somebody up. And, knowing Mark's shady-ass friends, they were scandalous enough to try and get him to do something to fuck us up. But I trusted him, because he didn't give me a reason not to. When he came home, I could tell when he'd had a good time and if he'd had too much to drink. I never checked his ass to see if anybody had gone there while he was out. Actually, I enjoyed the fact that brothers were checking him out, because at the end of the night, I knew who he was bringing that ass home to. I would sit up in bed waiting for him, either reading or watching television. He had rubbed off on me because he intro-duced me to British comedy, and I started to like that shit. At first, it was difficult to understand what the fuck they were say-ing, but as I got into it, it was funny as fuck.

I would hear him coming in and his keys hitting the table before he searched for me. As I lay in bed waiting for him, I could hear him taking his shoes off and walking up the stairs. He would throw himself on the bed, looking up at me. I could tell in his eyes he was happy to see me, as I was to see him. On moments like this, I dealt with the lingering cigarette smoke because my baby was home. He shared with me the events of the night and whether he'd had a good time or it was tired. I sometimes drifted back to my British television shows while he talked. I didn't want to hear about those bitches he went out with. Knowing that it would and could piss me off, he would roll over to me, searching for a kiss. He knew what he had to do. He was always in a playful mood after drinking. I knew I was going to tap it for him. He always teased me by straddling me, distracting me from the television and getting my dick hard. There were times I ignored the smell of smoke just to have him sooner, rather than later. Once he accomplished getting my dick hard, he would jump up and laugh, running to the bathroom to shower.

I yelled at him as I heard the shower running, "What the fuck you do that for?"

I could hear him laughing from the bathroom, as I prepared for what was to come.

When we decided to have a housewarming party, we invited both family and friends. By this time, both our fathers had passed and only our moms remained. In our individual lives, they were both aware we were gay and had met exes from both of our pasts. Our moms were both concerned about Mark and me for totally different reasons. When I shared the news with my mother about Mark being positive, I saw the fear in her eyes that maybe I was, and that was why we were together. It took a hell of a lot and a recent test result to convince her otherwise. When I took Mark home to meet her, she was quite reserved, almost off-putting. She grilled him like a cop, wanting to know everything about him. He passed with flying colors and even secured another invitation after he volunteered to wash dishes and clean up after dinner. When we left, she even kissed him and urged him to return.

When I met his mother, that was a different story. I thought I was dreaming at the openness this lady showered upon me. After hearing Mark's story, I knew she had been through a lot with him with bad relationships and broken hearts. I could only imagine the fear she felt in her heart of burying her only child before her, as a result of this disease. She must have sensed the joy in Mark's life, as well as hearing it daily when they chatted on the telephone. To her, I was her son's man. That was a title I claimed and wore with pride.

Our mutual friends shared in our joys of living and loving. There were times alone in the kitchen that one or two would ask how things were going, and I knew what they meant. They could see we were both happy, but their concern focused on Mark's health, and my ability to deal with his status. Sometimes it was easy to tell them I was cool; everything was great. At other times, I found myself flustered at the grilling. After awhile, they realized it was there and only Mark and I had to deal with it. And we did. The nights of lying in bed allowed us that private time to share our fears, hopes and dreams. It was the visitor that came and wasn't leaving. Like loved ones who were inconveniences at times, that's how we considered HIV. It was the visitor who wasn't going anywhere, so we learned how to co-exist with it.

Mark would sometimes trail off in our conversations late at night. Whether it was the meds, or the fatigue from the daily grind, I would lie there, holding him in my arms. He would sometimes moan in his sleep, and I would bend my ear closer to his lips to hear his words or chuckle at the conversations he had in his sleep. Also during these times, I found myself thinking of him. I had moments where I would see something or hear something about the disease that I wanted to share with him; some new "cure" in hopes of taking this thing away from him. It always turned out to be false hope. Lying in bed with Mark asleep, I counted my blessings. I believed in a God, but not in organized religion. These were moments that I could just share with myself and barter with God for a cure. I would sometimes get a little teary eyed at the thought of losing Mark to AIDS. I thought of how my life would be empty after fighting so hard for what I really wanted, now that I had it. Before my prayers, I would sometimes have silent arguments with my God, asking how He could allow this to happen, not only to Mark, but to the many others fighting the same fight. He never answered, but He shared with me what He needed me to know. His answer was lying in my arms. As I looked down at Mark's angelic face, totally peaceful, not fighting, I raised my face to heaven and thanked my God for the blessing He had brought to me.

MARK

Life was good. Everything I had hoped and had dreamed for had found its way into my life. After a lifetime of fighting the demons that were both tangible and intangible in my life, I was now on the winning team. Never in a million years, or the years I had existed on earth, did I think I would ever say I was happy. I loved my work, my family was well, and each day, my love for Kevin continued to grow. The days of lying in bed wondering what happiness was and whether it was attainable were now nightmares of the past. I even got to the point in my life, that I didn't allow my quarterly visits to dictate my feelings of living with HIV. In the couple of years Kevin and I had been together, we were thrown some curve balls in dealing with it. I knew the day would come when my doctor would inform me that I was diabetic. I had a family history of diabetes, and it was only a matter of time. I had avoided it for the longest time, but it became one more adjustment in my life. I added to my daily medication routine one lone pill to control the diabetes. I was fortunate not to have to inject myself with insulin. I had changed my eating habits since being diagnosed with HIV. The foods that nurtured me as a kid were now treats for good behavior or special moments. I didn't splurge or gorge on unhealthy foods. I wanted to beat both ailments that had found their way into my life and my body. If that wasn't enough, the side effects of the new HIV medications I had started taking recently had caused an increase in my cholesterol. It was a minor inconvenience, but each week, I filled the weekly supply of pills into the dispenser I kept at the side of my bed. Kevin rolled with the punches, even sometimes playing good cop/bad cop by patrolling what we both ate and drank. I had all but eliminated alcohol, outside of the occasional glass of wine reserved for special events. As the old saying goes, "When in Rome, do as the Romans do." I did. I followed the directions of my multiple healthcare providers, took care of myself, and did everything I was supposed to do. Unfortunately, over time, my best wasn't good enough.

I never allowed myself to think about my numbers when it came to my HIV disease. I had friends and met people who looked like athletes with less than 200 T cells, the cells that help fight off infections. There were times in which my own personal T cell count fluctuated and hovered at all-time lows, but I felt good and to me, that's all that mattered. Outside of common colds and that one year with the dreaded flu, I always bounced back. My numbers were never really high again after these battles, but my spirit was good and I felt good.

I was not going to complain to anyone about what was going on with me.

For the longest time, I was what some called a long-term non-progressor. I was HIV-positive and because of the fight I waged, I was able to keep it at bay. I was able to fend it off for the longest time, but my body started to show the effects of the disease.

My most recent visit to the doctor showed me exactly what was going on. He informed me, after my blood draw, that my T-cell count had dropped below 200. I was now officially diagnosed with AIDS. It was certainly a bitter pill to swallow, and harder information to share with Kevin when I got the news.

We attempted to ease each other's fear, saying it was probably a mistake, or it would be better the next go-around. He didn't have any concerns that he shared with me. That made me feel better about the situation. Nor did I show him the fear that was eating me up inside; I was a brave warrior. At least that's the face I showed him when he looked at me.

My immune system had taken a severe beating, and it had manifested itself in both test results and symptoms. What I thought were side effects of new medications were symptoms of the progressive disease. I found it difficult to keep my weight on and up, having to add an additional hole into my already stretched belt. The diarrhea limited my intimate moments with Kevin, as I became unable to control my bowels.

Over the last few weeks, I had been less than my normal self. I was a little more tired after work, to the point that I would head straight to bed until Kevin got home. Kevin would walk into the bedroom and sometimes catch me doubled over in pain from severe stomach cramps. This scared him as he went to retrieve a warm compress to apply to my head. I felt better when he lay down with me, but the pain and the lethargic feeling wouldn't subside. I promised him, at his request, to schedule a doctor's appointment. I presumed everything would eventually go away in time, but it didn't.

Like the early days of waiting for my test results, I eagerly waited for my doctor to call me and share what I hoped was good news. It was the late fall and the flu had started hitting folks early that year. I figured I had caught it from someone at work, and I would allow it to run its course. It wasn't the flu, as I suspected, or hoped.

Mycobacterium avium intracellulare, or MAC, as he told me, had come in and taken up room and board in my body. That explained the diarrhea, abdominal pains and weight loss. In addition to the drugs I took every night, I now had to add a heavy dose of antibiotics to the menu. My doctor informed me that, along with the current drugs, in order to prevent the re-occurrence of MAC, I would have to take them for the remainder of my days.

He leveled with me as he did each time I showed up for my appointments. With his quiet grace and having known me for the last twenty-plus years, he told me what I feared hearing: It didn't look good.

I knew this day would come and when it did, I thought I would be better prepared. The last few months, I had felt changes but kept these secrets to myself. Since Kevin and I had demanded honesty and communication with each other, this was the one thing I held close to my heart. It was unfair to keep the information from him, but I hoped that things would turn around. But they didn't.

I played off some of the changes he noticed in me; no one really knew me as well as he did. It was like the smallest thing that happened signaled him to question what was going on with me. In the few years we had been together, this was the first time I had ever lied to him.

I had some idea of how I would go out in a blaze of glory. I believed I would be there by myself, but now Kevin was here, and I didn't want to go anywhere. Life had been so fucking cruel to me. I believed God had kept me here on earth to punish me, make me suffer. And now my life was as perfect as I could imagine, and I wouldn't be able to stick around long enough to enjoy what I had hoped for all my life.

I stole a page from Juanita Moore's performance in the classic, *Imitation of Life*. I would take center stage as she did that last moment of her life. I would become the tragic *heroine*, surrounded by those I loved, sharing with each my true thoughts of how I wanted to be buried. That's what I thought when I found out I was positive; now, I wanted to live until the end of time.

No matter how much I wanted to keep the news from Kevin, I had to tell him. I needed to let him know, so that he could make the decision to be there. I couldn't allow him to die with me. I fought back the tears after my conversation with my doctor. I knew there would be many more to come later that evening.

The ride home seemed the longest on the Metro. I looked out the window into the dark cavernous tunnel, never wanting the ride to end. Once it did, Kevin would be there. I saw flashes of life in each light that brought me closer to home. I saw the first time I ever kissed a man. I saw the first time I ever cried over a man. I saw friends and family and the joy each one contributed to my life. I saw myself receiving my diagnosis. I saw Kevin. I saw the hopes and dreams we shared with each other. I saw how they seemed so vivid and real. Eventually, the clear images started to fade as I saw myself slowly disappearing from them. And there, at the last stop of my exit, I saw the image of Kevin standing alone. I was now only a passing dream.

As I exited the Metro, I dried my tears and hung my head low to avoid contact with anyone. I walked the few blocks home, thinking about Kevin's reaction. There would be no wonderful dinners this evening, or quiet moments of cuddling and watching television. Tonight, I would prepare him to say good-bye, as I prepared myself.

KEVIN

When I walked in the house, I could tell something was wrong. Usually when I arrived, I would find Mark in the kitchen deciding on dinner. The music from the radio would usually greet me before him, but tonight it was quiet. I heard something coming from upstairs and called out to him. He responded to let me know he was there. Lately, he hadn't been himself. He was in constant pain and there was a noticeable change in his weight and appearance. I lied to myself, pretending that everything he was experiencing was simply a minor bug. And as he had done in the past, he would get over this. But I was lying to make myself feel better. I didn't know exactly what the issue was, but I knew it was bad. I took away its power, by making light of the situation. I could see my baby get better in a matter of days, and we would continue loving each other.

I walked into the bedroom with Mark's back toward me. On the side of the bed, I saw a half-empty glass of wine. This was not a good sign. I slid into bed next to him to see how he was doing; I discovered he was crying. I didn't say anything, because his tears told me so much. I waited, reaching myself for the half-filled glass, to take a sip. I would need something stronger to deal with the blow of information I was sure he was going to finally tell me. I waited for him to find the courage to do so.

There were times in the past Mark and I had talked about his death. It was sometimes disturbing to hear conversation of him describing how and where he wanted to be buried. I would listen and agree, in order to move along the conversation, but he wanted me to understand. Death would become a reality, but I shoved it under the rug as he shared what songs and who he wanted to invite to his final resting. I became a bit uneasy and agitated at the discussion, finding a reason to remove myself from it. I couldn't do it this time.

I placed the glass back on the nightstand and grabbed him to face me. I noticed his eyes were bloodshot from the combination of wine and crying. His arms reached up toward my neck, bringing me closer to him. My heart was breaking for the answers I didn't want to hear.

As I held him, he avoided making eye contact with me while he told me what the doctor had said. By not looking at me, he couldn't see the hurt in my eyes. I held him closer as each word hit me harder and harder, and his hug was the only thing to soften the blow. While I was able to hold him and offer him my silent comfort, allowing him to say what he needed, I found very little solace and comfort for me. His words stopped making sense as I found anger in a God that would take him away from me. Each time he tried to face me to read what was on my face, I held him tighter. I didn't want to reveal to him what I was thinking.

I started to cuss God out in my head. There, I stood before Him, pleading for Him not to do this to me, to Mark. And this God said, "Thy will be done." As I followed Him, begging for more time, my words fell to the clouds before they reached His ears. *Why Mark? Why any of the other men and women? How many other lovers, husbands and wives had found themselves in the place where I now stood, making promises in order to keep the true love they searched for?* I felt Mark pull away to face me, and I instinctively altered my face to be compassionate, hiding all of the fear and anger that raged inside. He looked at me, searching my face to reveal what I was thinking, and I wiped his tears. Even through this difficult time, he was too concerned about me and what I was feeling to truly comprehend the severity of where his health had taken him. I continued to hold him for a while, allowing his tears to soak my shirt. There were moments of uncontrollable crying, to deafening silence. I needed a moment to myself to digest the words he shared with me. And my escape would have to come in the form of our brief separation.

I removed myself from his embrace and headed to the bathroom to run a hot bath for him. Usually, Mark would take a shower before heading to bed, but I ran a hot bath, adding the eucalyptus oil he liked. He wasn't up to eating, but I was adamant about putting food in him now more than ever. I told him that I would run out and grab something to bring back so we wouldn't have to cook. That was my excuse, at least, to get out of the house for a moment. I raised him from the bed, removing the now loose-fitting clothes from his body, and guided him to the bathroom. We kept a radio in the bathroom for morning showers, and I turned the dial to something soothing to help him relax. He had to run a little more cold water in the tub to cut the heat. I watched him as he submerged slowly into the water. I could get him to stay there for a while by retrieving the wine from the bedroom. I placed the glass in his hand and asked what he craved for dinner. He fought me by saying he wasn't hungry, but dammit, he was going to eat tonight and every morning, noon and night from now on. After telling me it didn't matter, I excused myself, rushing to deal with the sickness building in my throat and thoughts of losing him.

The cold air hit me with a rush and snapped my thoughts in half. I needed some time to process the information. Driving would have been so much quicker to get to a place to grab something. But I opted to walk. I slowed my pace as I pondered my life without Mark. There were times where we walked the same path to the grocery store together to enjoy quiet moments and talks. We commented on getting a dog after seeing neighbors on beautiful mornings walking theirs. We would think about the size, color and name for our "child." That thought eventually ended, after watching the owners bend down and pick up shit with a plastic bag. With that image, I thought about me having to clean Mark's shit. There had been brothers who had "accidents" of releasing their bowels while I was fucking them, and I was repulsed by the thought and the smell. But I would never feel that way about Mark. He would not be able to control it. And it broke my heart to think of me having to treat him like a baby and wipe his ass.

I slowed my pace because I wanted more time alone. I thought of the brothers I knew for a fact that had died, and how this disease had fucked them up. It wasn't pretty, by any means. For a moment, I wanted Mark to die in order to prevent his body and spirit from taking a turn for the worse. If my God had any fucking mercy, He wouldn't make him suffer. But I didn't really want that. I wanted him to live. I wanted him to continue to love me.

I stopped at one of the local neighborhood bars to get a drink. I fucking needed it. I had no one to call and share what I was feeling, or the thoughts in my head. I found the comfort I needed in the bottom of the shot glass. I didn't have to fight for the bartender's attention as I raised a finger, alerting him that my glass was empty. Sometimes bartenders could tap into your psyche and discern when it was a good time to engage in small talk for a bigger tip. This wasn't one of them.

Within a matter of minutes, I felt like I had finished a bottle of shots. My fears continued to grab hold of me. I didn't think Mark would try to kill himself while I was gone, but if he did, I could understand why. The last thing I wanted to do was walk in and see his body floating in the bathtub. I quickly threw some money on the bar and headed home. I quickened my pace to the door, empty handed without the food I had promised.

I ran upstairs to the bathroom and noticed he was not there. I leaped to the bedroom to see that he had claimed his side of the bed in a semi-fetal position. We rarely, if at all, wore more to bed at night than a T-shirt, but he was there bundled in pajamas and his robe. I took my place next to him in bed and once again, I held him. I took a cue from him and did what I needed to do; I began to cry.

I began to let out everything that cluttered my head and my heart. I held him closer, as he pulled me closer to him. My tears fell like a flowing river, hitting his freshly bathed skin. He remained silent, as he allowed me this moment to release my fears through my sobs. All this time in our relationship, I thought I was the stronger of the two, but it was his silent stroking of my arm that showed me who possessed the most strength. I continued to bawl, as he encouraged me to let it all out. He probably could tell that I had been drinking, but he didn't say a word. I didn't know how else to cope with the news he had given me. I found myself cussing God up one side and down the other. Then for measure, I threw in the motherfucker who had infected Mark. I wished, at that moment, I could get my hands around his fucking neck to choke what life he had and the life he was taking from me. I cried until I couldn't cry anymore, feeling spent and exhausted. I continued to hold Mark, and he continued to offer me a promise he couldn't keep, "It's going to be alright."

MARK

We took the next couple of days off from work and stayed in the house. I found it very difficult to get out of bed because of the way I was feeling and the emotional upheaval in my life. Kevin and I maintained conversation sporadically, but I could tell he was dealing with his own shit as well. He wasn't a very good cook when we started dating and when we moved in together, but he had mastered a few meals. When I was too drained or exhausted to get out of bed, he was in the kitchen banging pots and pans to fix me something to eat. We were used to eating at the table, but the last couple of days found us eating meals in bed. We replayed the doctor's comments and concerns over and over. I guess Kevin thought maybe I had missed telling him something, and that maybe that missing word or sentence would hold some wonderful cure to this thing. But each time I shared with him, the story stayed the same. And each time he looked defeated.

When he came home the other night, supposedly from going to get dinner for us, I could smell the liquor on his breath. I wanted to talk to him about that and why he felt he needed to go drinking, but I didn't. When he crawled into bed with me and held me, his sobs told me everything he needed to.

As the time for our self-imposed exile from the world came closer to an end, and we both needed to report to work, we finally talked. Once again, he asked what the doctor said and like rewinding the tape, I replayed the message for him.

When he asked how I was feeling, I knew he meant well, but my fear came out in the form of hostility. "How do you think I feel? I am dying and there is nothing I can fucking do about it."

Of all the arguments we'd had in the past, Kevin never backed down from me once, but this time he cowered and allowed me to be angry. I quickly apologized to him because it wasn't his fault. He didn't do this to me and he didn't deserve what I was giving him. If anything, he was guilty of loving me more than anyone ever had. I reached for his face to touch the growth of facial hair from the last couple of days. Rather than argue and say something I would regret later, we sat down and had a true heart-to-heart conversation. I was scared. I knew the disease would take control of me. Kevin allowed me to share with him what I wanted to do next in the time we had left. Without hesitation, he agreed to everything. We went about making our last moments together something that we would both remember for the rest of our lives.

Like Juanita Moore's Annie, I reached for a notepad I kept on my side of the bed and a pen. I handed it to Kevin to jot down what my wishes would be for that moment when it was time to say good-bye. It was not only our fears we shared, but the fears my mother would have to deal with during this difficult time. I made Kevin promise me that if this was too much for him to bear, that he would leave. I couldn't ask him to go through this with me. It was not his fight, nor was it his issue to deal with. If he was unable to see this through, as much as it would hurt, I would certainly understand. I always had a back-up plan for this moment. The timing would be difficult for my mother, so I was able to recruit long-time friends who would take a lot off of her to ensure my wishes were met.

Kevin wouldn't hear any of it. He assured me that he was going to be there with me, through it all. I attempted to smile, looking to see if what he said would be betrayed by what he truly felt.

KEVIN

S ome of Mark's requests were a bit out there, so much so that I had to reel him in. He made light of the fact, by saying he wanted to be propped up in his casket so his spirit could see who attended the funeral. I thought that was a bit morbid; he laughed. The other items on his list were easier to embrace. Of course, he wanted us to spend time with our families. We hadn't quite broken the news to our mothers, but we agreed that we would do something special for them for a weekend. Neither had been to New York, and we decided to book a trip there to show them the town.

I was reluctant in agreeing to participate with him having another "Celebration of Life" party. I wanted to spend what time we had together with just the two of us. It wasn't like he was given a date and time of his pending death; I knew this celebration was something he had to do. He wanted to have it soon before he took a turn for the worse. Our friends wouldn't recognize how much he had changed. Everything was coming full circle, as I thought back to the first time I met him at the party a number of years ago.

It wouldn't be a big bash like the one he held when we met, so we agreed on a small group of friends, and set the date. Our conversation continued to run the range of emotions, laughing about some of his requests, to the one request that broke my heart.

In the past, we had talked about this moment. If anything happened to either of us, we agreed the other would be responsible for following out all requests. My mother was a staunch believer in burial plots, as was Mark's. But Mark changed his mind about being buried. It wasn't the thought of death that bothered him now, but the cost. We were both financially secure, but he didn't want to waste the money being buried in a box six feet under. He wanted to be cremated. When he said this, I couldn't imagine having his ashes in this place we called home to remind me of his absence. But he had other wishes to accompany the cremation.

He wanted his ashes distributed to his family and friends. Each one would have a piece of him wherever they would go. He wanted each to receive a small vial of his remains, and a year after his death, to release him wherever they were and let him go. I couldn't go on with this conversation; it seemed so final. I knew it was, but it was too much for me to handle. I quickly agreed to it, to avoid discussing it anymore, but he wouldn't leave it there.

He told me that, in time, I would love again. He wanted me to hold on to his remains, the ashes, until I found someone else.

This time, I became angry. "You think this is all about you. I am hurting, listening to this shit. Believe me, baby, I know you need to do this, but this is fucking killing me." I got up from the bed to go look out the window. I felt that same feeling I had when I came home from work and he gave me the information. "I am trying my damndest to be strong, but I can't. All the time I fought trying not to love you because of my fucked-up reservations about you being positive, I am now fighting so fucking hard to keep you here with me. It's not fair. I have been kicking myself in the ass, for not following my heart from the very beginning, and now I am going to lose you. This is fucked up."

I turned to him, facing him and showing how much I was hurting. He looked at me with a blank stare. He knew the toll it took on me, but he wanted me to face the fact that he was leaving me, not because he wanted to, but because it was time for him to go. I looked out the window again, searching for this fucking God to give me a sign, or to strike me down to put an end to this. The sun shone brightly in my eyes as a symbol of this God's love. He replaced my fears with compassion. He wiped my tears with His gentle hand and He granted me strength to return to the bed, and to Mark. I grabbed the notepad and pushed my feelings aside for the time being, to make my baby happy, for whatever it was worth.

MARK

It was the beginning of the end for me. I wasn't getting any better, and I had no false sense that some kind of miracle would save me. Believe it or not, I found peace in knowing I had done the very best I could with handling my circumstances. Within a few weeks of our discussion, Kevin was a trooper, putting everything into play. We held the party as I watched everyone look at me with concern. Kevin and I never confirmed for anyone outside of our families what was going on. There were whispers throughout the night, but for us, it was a time of quiet celebration. This would be the last time I would see most of them.

The trip to New York with our mothers was bittersweet. Before going, Kevin and I got the two of them together to discuss my condition. There were lots and lots of tears shed. I couldn't help but think about my mother when we sat down and talked. She had been through so much with me, and now her biggest fear was coming true. She was a strong woman and because of her strength, I was able to face this head on. Between our two moms, when their schedules permitted, one or the other would come to visit Kevin and me, to prepare meals to help me maintain the dwindling weight or to take up the slack of housecleaning. Kevin spent the majority of his time focused on me and taking care of me. When my energy level was good, we made the trip to New York and checked out a show on Broadway and visited Harlem. We had a great time, even when it took so much for me to go. It was one of the great memories I wanted to leave each of them with.

Our bathroom began to look like the local pharmacy, as the medications I needed to take increased more and more. The fresh floral scents I used to air out the house on the weekends was now replaced with cleaners that left strong scents to control the smell of sickness. Kevin took on more responsibilities as I focused my energy on getting up and taking my meds daily. I was weakened by the side effects and was increasingly confined to bed. When Kevin was at work, I found myself wanting to put an end to all of this. I sometimes thought about taking all the medications at once and committing suicide, but it would be unfair to Kevin, for him to come home and find me like that. In those times I was alone, I would cry about where I was in life and with this disease. I would beat myself up thinking about where I had gone wrong and how I could have done things differently. But my God had a way of kicking you in your ass. During those moments of sad self-reflection, He would place his hand on my heart and open my eyes to the wonderful gift of love He had granted me. I would see Kevin's face and reminisce about all the wonderful times we shared. Even though I had no sex drive, I thought about the first time Kevin and I had made love. The beauty of that moment remained with me all this time. I managed to hug myself, holding on to the thoughts of his arms around me. I believed in my heart, that no matter where I ended up in the afterlife, I could take those memories with me.

Kevin made sure never to leave me alone during the day. If he wasn't there on extended lunch hours, I was never at a loss for friends and co-workers who stopped by to check on me and keep me company. Each one, in their own way, tried to take my mind off of the battle within my body. But each time, I was either rushing to the bathroom or too tired to really entertain or enjoy the company. I had taken to wearing adult diapers to make sure that none of them would have to aid me with any accidents. Kevin started getting up earlier each morning to help me with showering or bathing, in the event visitors would stop by. With some, they treated me like the old Mark, laughing and joking, cutting up as if we were still in the clubs, cruising and taking shots at the customers who threw lame-ass, come-on lines. It was moments like this, very rare moments, that took my mind off of everything, albeit briefly. On the other hand, I felt the tension from some, who were only there as a favor at Kevin's request. Sensing their uneasiness, I would quickly dismiss them and their fucking pity. I would stress that I was tired and needed to rest. They took this as a way out without guilt. I could tell those who were uncomfortable before they left. I could hear the water running from the bathroom or the kitchen, scrubbing off a disease they thought they could catch by simply helping me up the stairs to my bedroom.

KEVIN

With everything that was going on, I tried to maintain a brave front for Mark. In the few moments we spent apart, I kept hoping I would awaken from this bad dream. If I wasn't at work, I was constantly by his side, playing nurse-maid and loving partner. My heart was breaking, and there was nothing I could do. I wasn't focusing at work and my performance was suffering. My boss, who knew about Mark and me, called me into her office to discuss what was going on. She was not only my supervisor, but a good friend to the two of us. Of course, she commented on how my work was suffering, but she was more concerned about how I was doing. She told me what Mark was going through was in God's hands and she was more concerned about me. After a long discussion and some shuffling of work, we agreed that for the time being, I would be able to work from home to tend to Mark. He was getting progressively worse and my thoughts were constantly with him.

I was able to get friends to stop by and check on him when I was unable to do it, but after they left, he would share how uncomfortable some of them were. Motherfuckers. Mark was fine to be around when he was the life of the party or living and looking like nothing was wrong, but the first time these bitches had to step up and be a friend, they found it difficult to do that. When he shared these events with me, I mentally removed those bastards from the list of those who genuinely cared. In abiding by his wishes for the trips and party he wanted done, it had taken a lot out of him. I noticed also that the meds were really fucking with him. What I found interesting was the meds that were supposed to help him live provided debilitating side effects. I wished I could have taken away his pain. Hell, I wished I could have taken away the disease.

I now had a makeshift office at home in the spare room we used for storage. While he rested during the day, watching soaps or enjoying the videos I rented for him, it felt good to be with him, just a few feet away. I would take breaks to check in on him to see if he needed anything. I would sometimes lie down with him and get caught up in whatever drama Mrs. Chancellor and Jill were getting into. I even went so far as to get a little bell for him to beckon for me, if he needed me.

Depending on his mood, Mark would sometimes make it down the stairs to sit in the living room. He would greet and entertain the visitors and friends who had stopped by, bearing gifts and food for his consumption. Our refrigerator was stocked with more than enough Tupperware containers with his favorites to maintain his weight. By now, he had lost his appetite for anything. After reading some reports, I encouraged him to smoke a little reefer to increase his appetite for food, which would help with his eating habits. The miracle of weed worked for a bit on two fronts: it allowed him to eat something, and it helped with the nausea caused by the medications. The smell didn't bother me, because I knew it was helping to keep him alive.

On the few days I had to go into the office to turn in a report or attend a meeting, there was always someone present to keep Mark company and to do his bidding. I was determined not to leave him alone in his condition. I was only half present at work when I attended meetings; my thoughts and concerns were at home with him. I would spend an extra minute or two to play catch-up with co-workers before bolting out of the door to return home to him.

One day, after returning home, one of those whom we called friends informed me that Mark had had a bad day. Now, he was asleep, as the friend and I sat down at the table. Everyone had been supportive during this difficult time. I was sure they had shared conversations on how we, or rather how I, could do what I was doing. They never had the nerve to share their thoughts with me, with the exception of this one.

I didn't realize what was being said behind my back. I felt the anger build as he asked me how I could do it. He didn't have the guts to give an inch of what I was doing for Mark. And I snapped.

All the anger I felt, all the hurt I was keeping inside, came out as I read him about his remarks. How could I do this? It was easy; I loved this man. He was my heart, and fuck anybody who had anything to say about what I was doing and how I was doing it. Sissies were getting on my fucking nerves, commenting on shit they didn't know anything about or understand. Before he could apologize for his comment, I slammed the door in his face.

I went upstairs to check on Mark and noticed he was sound asleep. I'm glad my outburst had not awakened him. I placed a gentle kiss on his forehead and headed back downstairs to think about the conversation I'd had with this so-called friend.

I sat there thinking how many of "our" friends felt the way he did about Mark and me. How many of them thought about walking out on him at this time in his life? It was all so fucked up to think that we love people long enough to satisfy what we need them for. I thought back to all of the times that I had fought my feelings for Mark, and how his disease would eventually tear us apart. Now, as I sat there, there was no place I would rather have been. It was hard, God knows it was, but I wasn't going anywhere. If we spent half our time loving because of what we felt, versus what others think, can you imagine how many folks who lived with this disease wouldn't be alone at this trying time? I realized that I was where I was supposed to be. I only wished I had met Mark earlier so that we could have had more time together. But I was blessed, knowing that I was able to share just a small part of his life with him. I was the lucky one.

I counted my blessings for this gift that had come into my life. The anger that I felt for this God of Gods had subsided. He had granted me peace for the remainder of this journey. I wasn't into praying, but in the quiet of that office, I got down on my knees. I thanked God for Mark and for all of the trials and tribulations. I thanked Him for a love so pure and beautiful, that if I never found it again in life, I was blessed that He had given it to me once in my lifetime. I prayed for Mark also. I prayed that my God, Mark's God, would ease the pain of his disease. I didn't want him to suffer; I wanted him to feel the same peace I felt with the journey. I thanked God once again for showing me His light, but also showing me Mark's light.

MARK

As much as I avoided mirrors in the house, it was hard not to recognize the dramatic change in appearance I now possessed. I didn't recognize myself anymore. My body had taken a severe beating from complications and weight loss. Dealing with thrush, and other ailments, had added to my low sense of self. But no matter how badly I felt, Kevin was there for me. I could tell things had taken their toll on him as well. He showed signs of weight loss from the stress and around-the-clock care of me. I wanted to tell him to walk away and preserve himself, but he wouldn't listen. I didn't want to be selfish; this was my battle. I could have easily thrown in the towel and moved back to my mom's in order to have someone to take care of me. There I would have around-the-clock care from her as well as family. At the suggestion was made to Kevin, I was met with an adamant no; it wasn't going to happen. I couldn't argue or disagree because I didn't have much fight in me. The remaining strength I had was reserved to battle the daily struggles of climbing the stairs, or trying to force food down. The reefer made things easy as it took me to different places to focus on. I could lose myself for the brief time that the THC took control of my thoughts; it was relaxing and calming.

As it became more and more difficult to climb the stairs, Kevin surprised me one day by purchasing a recliner to put in the bedroom. I was now confined to the four walls of our bedroom. The recliner allowed me moments to sit up comfortably as he changed the sheets because of accidents or night sweats I had encountered. He never made me feel bad about these things. He would open the blinds for the sunlight to peek in and warm me; he had taken control of everything now.

When he spent time in the office, I would focus on the one thing that would leave my mark—my last will and testament. I didn't have many possessions, and Kevin and I agreed whatever was left over from the cremation would be shared between him and my mom. Neither wanted to hear talk like this, but in my solitude, I wrote out my last thoughts. I decided to leave to my little cousins the gift of music. I had always been a lover of great vocalists who could deliver on the lyrics they were given. The music of recent play had become nothing more than studio singers who lacked the talent and wherewithal to maintain a recording career. I wanted the youth in my family to be able to put a classic Nancy Wilson album on the turntable and think of me.

When my grandmother passed away, I was given her wedding band to celebrate her life. She was someone truly special to me, and this ring would serve as a continued reminder and bond between Kevin and me. Rather than wait for my afterlife, I decided I would present it to him before my passing.

The other possessions would be donated to local AIDS service organizations, including clothes, books and the like. There were special mementos I thought of as I wrote out this will, keeping in mind who should receive what, and how much of it they would get.

Marriage was a no-no in our community. As much as gays and lesbians wanted to share in the same unions as straights, we were relegated to backyard confessions of our love for one another.

My union with Kevin didn't need to be defined by a piece of paper to show that we once loved, and continued to love, as our counterparts. But I wanted to carry something with me in my afterlife.

I also decided to take a moment and write Kevin a letter. It would be my voice, my heart, and my love, speaking to him beyond my grave. As I wrote out the words, I felt the tears fall, staining the ink on the paper, smudging my words, but never questioning my heart. I neatly tucked the letter away in a folder that I hid from Kevin. I sealed it, with special instructions written on the envelope, not to be opened until a year after my death.

I called out to Kevin to join me in the bedroom. I assured him everything was okay; I just wanted to see him and ask him a question. He knelt beside me, waiting for the question.

I stroked his face and asked, "Will you marry me?"

Asked and answered.

KEVIN

There was no hesitation when Mark asked me to marry him. If we lived in a society that embraced same-sex marriages, I would have done it a long time ago. Mark didn't like using the term "husband," as white gay men used. We decided on "partners." Calling ourselves "lovers" only led folks to focus on what we did in bed. I called off work for the rest of the day as we sat down to plan our wedding. We agreed it would be small and intimate and held in our home. We both agreed that casual wear was the way to go, since Mark was unable to fit in the suits he once wore. We got on the telephone to call the few invitees who had stuck with us and had embraced our union. Everyone was happy and volunteered their time to help us. The moms both agreed to take care of the food, and some friends would handle the food and wine set-up. I reached out to a girl-friend of ours, who had pipes, and requested a special tribute as my gift to Mark. She cried on the telephone and said she would be honored. All I had to do was show up.

That night, with all the excitement of this sharing of my love of Mark with family and friends, I was unable to sleep. As I had done every night since we'd been together, I held me tightly. I looked out the window, staring at the stars, and sent a silent prayer through the night air to my God. I asked for just a little more time to share this life with Mark. I went further and selfishly asked for Mark to have one good day of health, to stand beside me for this special moment. I prayed as I had never prayed before. *Dear God, just a little more time.*

We couldn't have asked for a better day for the ceremony. It was bitterly cold outside, but our home was filled with life and love. I sensed Mark was a bit insecure about the way he looked, but there was something beautiful about him this day. He had a glow about him, and the color had come back in his face. He was much smaller, but he was still the same man I had fallen in love with.

Mark had to rely on the assistance of a cane when he walked down the stairs to greet our extended family for the ceremony. They didn't shy away from extending hugs or kisses because of how he looked now. They all felt like me; they were happy to be here. We created our own version of a service. There was no pomp and circumstance, no candles burning—simply an overflowing of our love for one another.

We both agreed to share our words with each other and the attendees; call it makeshift vows. I noticed Paula from the church I attended on occasion, and smiled at the surprise she and I had discussed for this moment. I had extended an invitation for her to join us for this celebration, and Mark was oblivious to why she was there. As we stood before family and friends, Mark braced himself against me for support. I agreed to go first with my speech because I wasn't much for public speaking. Before I could start, I whispered in Mark's ear I had a special gift from me. At that moment, Paula stepped forward to present us with the gift of song.

As tears welled up in her eyes, she sang the most beautiful a capella rendition of Gladys Knight's "The Best Thing that Ever Happened to Me" that I had heard. Mark looked at me and mouthed along silently with Paula as she shouted from the rafters, reminiscent of her solos at church:

"... for every moment that I've spent hurting
There was a moment that I spent, ah just loving you"

Paula's voice and the lyrics pierced my heart as I looked at Mark. I felt the joy and the pain of our love in that one verse. It summed up so much of what we had been through. If Mark could have, I know that he would have sung the words himself, but he needed help. He had never looked more beautiful to me as he did at that moment. Between the tears, I stopped time long enough to hold on to that memory for the rest of my life.

When Paula finished, there wasn't a dry eye in the house. I had to clear my throat and come back into the moment as I replayed the verse in my head. I sniffled, preventing the snot from coming out of my nose. I reached in my pocket to retrieve the notes I had jotted down for this moment. I quickly looked at them and realized what I was feeling; I didn't need notes to remind me. I placed them back in my pocket and spoke from my heart.

"You, Mark, have been the greatest gift my life has been blessed with. For a time there, I fought and struggled with infor- mation you gave, only to realize I loved you because of you. You became my teacher. I learned from you how to let go and let love. You became my best friend, allowing me to be myself, embracing all my flaws, and we know I had many. You became my partner, allowing me to share this journey with you, and you never once made it a dull trip. You showed me that patience and communication are the keys to any successful relationship. I can't begin to tell you, or show you, what your love has meant to me, but from my heart to yours, I hope you know it."

I reached out my hand to my mother, waiting for the ring that I had purchased for Mark. His fingers were much smaller than I remembered, but I promised him I would have the ring resized for him. With tears in her eyes, my mother placed her hands on both of ours, silently granting her approval of our union.

She leaned forward to cup Mark's face in her hands, tears clouding her vision, whispering, "I love you, son."

Mark inhaled deeply, returning the kiss and the smile of approval. He redirected his eyes to mine, thanking me for the ring. But his eyes said so much more he couldn't say; they thanked me for this moment.

MARK

I knew how difficult it was for Kevin to show his feelings in front of everyone there, but he spoke as if we were the only two people in the room. I was still wiping my eyes from Paula's song and holding back from the tender words Kevin had shared before I spoke mine.

I grabbed Kevin's hand and held it tightly, as I stood there waiting for my turn. "I love you. We go through life looking and searching for someone to love, and to love us in return. When I wasn't looking, you found me. You showed your fear, but it didn't rule you because you are still here. You showed your strength when others would have run away. You are the dream I dreamed of all my life, and for once, my dream came true." I felt my energy slipping away, but I wanted to continue. I reached into my pocket to grab my grandmother's ring and placed it on Kevin's finger. I reached for his face and kissed his cheek. "Thank you for traveling this road with me and keeping me company." I caught myself choking up again and concluded my thoughts, "Thank you for closing the door to my fears and opening my heart to loving again." With my final words, my mother, who stood beside me, holding me up as well, placed her hands on both mine and Kevin's. With the same rush of emotion, she confirmed and acknowledged our union.

We hugged as our loved ones raised a toast to our "marriage."

I never thought it could happen, but then again, I wasn't sure about a lot of things in my life. The only thing I knew at that moment was I was in love, and love was in love with me.

We celebrated with a dance and cheers and support. My heart was overflowing with both joy and sadness as I faced the fact; this was the last time I would see all of my loved ones together in one room. I hid this sad realization from others as I continued to bask in the notion that I was a married man. I didn't want to show anyone how my energy was slipping, but I endured. Kevin held me in his arms, and we danced the sweetest lovers' dance.

KEVIN

Mark and I decided to take a pseudo honeymoon, which consisted of a weekend trip to West Virginia. It wasn't the typical place black gay men went to, but there was a nice little cabin in the woods where we spent our last weekend together. It was a time to share this last moment together, living and loving for the time we were afforded. The cabin itself was drafty, but the fireplace made up for it. Mark settled in front of the fireplace as I got everything going. Within a matter of minutes, the glow of the fire warmed him as I went about unpacking the groceries we had bought for the weekend. I checked the bedroom to make sure it was warm enough for him and noticed the welcomed addition of another fireplace. I got it roaring and closed the door to keep the warmth confined until we were ready to adjourn for the evening.

He didn't have much of an appetite, but he attempted to put something in his stomach. It was light, but it was healthy, and I was happy to see he had tried, at least for my sake.

The bathroom had a spacious bathtub for two, and I ran a scalding hot bath for us. I lit the candles and we relaxed after the long trip. It was great to be secluded from the world and pretend everything had stopped for us. But our reality was far from that. Time was not on our side. We continued to remain silent, thankful for this bittersweet moment. As the water started to cool, I got out first to dry off and help Mark out of the tub. I allowed him to dry himself while I checked the fire in the bed-room. It was still roaring as he dressed and found his way into the room. On the way up to the cabin, we had stopped at a general store for supplies, and I came across a cassette tape with the Gladys Knight's greatest hits. I placed it on the counter along with my other purchases.

There was a little boom box reserved for those who rented the cabin. I slipped the tape in, cueing it to our song. We both con-sented to sipping a little champagne to celebrate our union, without overdoing it.

With the fire serving as our spotlight, I pressed play and reached for my man's hand, slowly lifting him into my arms. I was gentle with him as I placed my arms around him and shared our last dance together. Gladys sang to our hearts, celebrating with us and leaving us with memories. We didn't need to speak a word to each other, for our hearts did all the talking. It was a moment to celebrate the love we shared; it was also the begin-ning of saying good-bye.

MARK

Two weeks had passed since Kevin and I had returned from the cabin in West Virginia. No matter what I did, my condition got worse. I was put back on Sustiva, and even after using it in the past, I still encountered the unbearable side effects. My dreams were always windows to my soul, and with Sustiva, I was able to place myself in those dreams each and every night.

Since we returned, there was a certain peace that had come over me. I was ready to go home, but something was holding me back. As I slept at night, I found myself stepping into this one dream that recurred each night. It contained flashbacks of my life—the good, and the sometimes bad. Each time I would awaken at the same place, the same step, searching the same passing faces. The dream ended for me, where the reality of life had stepped in a number of years ago. It was as if my life had come full circle, and now, I was living in the last few minutes of my reality.

I got out of bed this one morning because the sheets were soaked from yet another experience of night sweats. My feet ached from the neuropathy that had set in. As I swung my legs out of bed to place them onto the floor, the slightest pressure applied to them made me feel like I was walking on a bed of nails. I reached for the cane next to my bed that had become my constant companion and walking aid. I was careful not to disturb Kevin while he slept. The last two weeks, my dreams had awakened him, and now today, of all days, he was able to sleep peacefully.

I made my way down the hallway to the linen closet to retrieve a sheet to cover my side of the bed. When Kevin got up, he would feel the dampness and change the sheets, as he had done numerous times these last weeks. I stopped by the bathroom and turned the lights on. I squinted from their brightness. I ran the water in the basin to cool the sweat and took notice of the man in the mirror looking back at me. I didn't recognize him anymore. He was the skeletal remains of someone once called pretty. I didn't want to stare too long as my heart was broken facing him. Yes, my life had come full circle.

I decided to grab the robe hanging behind the bathroom door instead of changing the sheets. I slowly made my way back to the bedroom to rest. I eased myself down into the recliner Kevin had purchased for me some time ago and watched him as he slept. I traced the curves of his body to take with me on my next journey. There were so many memories of him—too many to choose from—but this was one I would treasure forever. I looked at the bed where we had shared many good times and bad times. I saw the two of us making love; I saw us watching television. I saw him crying. I saw life and love within these four walls. And now it was time to say good-bye.

I was careful not to disturb him as I took him in. In my life, I had experienced many joys and defeats. The highlights of my life, played out in my thoughts, overshadowing all of the bad that I had allowed into my world. For each moment that was something special, I was able to snip it at the right time, to create a montage of the wonderful life I had lived. It wasn't always pretty, but nothing in life is always that wonderful. But for the travels of my mind and heart, I was able to weed through all of the bad and see all of the beauty I possessed and shared with others.

I saw the moments of growing up as a little boy, running with my cousins, sharing Grandma's cooking and stories that nurtured us into adulthood. I saw Mom's beaming light, my angel here on earth, as she was sent to guide me along the way. At times, she would withhold information on the journey, only to silently show me and lead me to where I was destined to be. I saw all of the old boyfriends I had loved and whom I thought had loved me. Our paths were brought together for a reason, whether it was to open the door to those who truly loved us, or to leave us with a message they were sent to deliver. I watched myself grow from that little boy, into a grown man, living and loving, learning and teaching, celebrating through the tears to discover the true me. At times, the lessons were hard, but I was wiser and stronger because of them.

Mentally, during those snippets of my memories, I was able to step inside the dream and thank each one for the gift they had brought to my life. There was no need to hold on to bitterness or hurtful feelings; I was able to see and experience the light at the end of the tunnel. It was because of those traveling companions, I became the Mark that I was always supposed to be.

I also saw him along the journey. The one who had stolen my life from me. He was not the gaunt-looking man who had apologized to me after infecting me with HIV. He was vibrant and beautiful as ever. Once again, he had apologized. I could have taken this moment to turn this trip down memory lane into a nightmare, but for some strange reason, I thanked him as I hugged him. I thanked him for closing the door of my love for him and allowing me to find what was later down the road for me: my blessing, my Kevin. Some would have thought to take the moment to cuss and yell, but as we talked, I took responsibility for my own actions. I watched him walk away as I continued, and he assured me the journey was only beginning.

I said good-bye to the friends and club-hopping buddies who shared many a drink and dances with me. We smiled and raised one last toast to life. I asked them to remember me in dance, on those nights when partners are scarce—think of me and I am there twirling with the best.

As the trip came closer to the end, and the road was running out, there, waiting for me, was Kevin. The crisp, white linen pants and shirt contrasted with his dark ebony features. The road was soft on my bare feet as he reached out his hand toward me. On his finger, shining in the bluest of skies, was my grandmother's wedding band, which was now his. Behind his back was a mirror that he allowed me to look into. There was no sign of disease or death on my face.

He whispered in my ear, "This allows you to see the true beauty that I was graced with." He smiled as he hugged me. There were no tears. He gently kissed me and urged me forward. There was nothing left to see, there was nothing left to long for, because the journey had ended. I hesitated to step forward, but Kevin encouraged me. I looked back to see him fading before me. "It's okay, baby, it's okay. I love you."

My journey had come to an end.

KEVIN

I heard him slowly getting out of bed as I moved to feel the wetness from his side of the bed. I could tell it was that damn dream again. He told me about it, but he never really shared the details of it. It had disturbed this moment for him yet again. I could have easily gotten up to change the sheets, or gotten the robe for him, but that felt like taking away his last bit of independence. I watched him as he headed out the bedroom to make sure he didn't fall on his way.

When I heard him returning, I closed my eyes quickly to see him pass me as he entered and slinked down in the chair I had gotten him. I could hear the squeak from the hinges as he tried to quietly situate himself in the chair. I faked the moment of waking up to turn around and see him staring out the window. The sun was slowly rising, hitting his eyes, and showing the most vibrant shade of brown I had never noticed before. His eyes told me that he was tired. I called out to him, but he didn't respond. He continued to stare into space with a certain calmness that claimed his attention. I jumped up, scared of what was happening. I called out again, breaking his concentration, as he looked at me and smiled.

I wasn't ready for this, but I knew I had to let him go. I only asked that he allow me to hold him for a moment. I walked toward him, picking him up and carrying him to bed. I replaced our positions now, me in the dampness of his spot, him warming in mine. I sat up with my back slightly against the headboard and brought his body to mine. His face was now resting on my chest as I held him. I could hear and feel his gasps for breath—labored and long. I looked down, asking with my eyes if he was okay, and he smiled back at me before closing his. He opened them once again to answer. This was not the time to spend on words. I wanted to call the doctor, the ambulance, somebody, anybody, but he wouldn't allow me.

His breathing became more rapid as I felt him slipping away from me. His body was no longer tense from the daily pain he experienced. I felt the heaves in my chest go up and down, fighting back the sobs forming. His small frame rose with mine as I felt tears start to stream down my face. He gently kissed my chest, feeling my tears wash over him. He took his tiny hand and reached toward my eyes to dry them. Much like him, I felt his life slipping away from me. I lowered myself to be close to him one last time, still allowing the breaths to signal me that he was still with me.

I faced him as he looked at me, crying. They were not tears of sadness, but of relief. I bit my lip as I continued crying myself and nodded, *It's okay, baby, I'm here*. I held him closer to me one last time and kissed him gently.

With one last nod, I told him once again, "It's okay." Knowing I had to let him go, he smiled and closed his eyes. I whispered what my heart had known all the time, but took a while for me to catch up to, "I love you."

One Year Later
KEVIN

I lay in bed the morning of the anniversary of Mark's death. I didn't have it in me to face the day knowing he had been gone a year. I remembered holding him all day when he died, refusing to let anyone enter and break the bond we had. His body, over the course of the day, stiffened and became cold. It didn't matter. I continued to rock him, hoping that he would return to me. But he was gone. I cried until there was nothing left in me. Removing him from my arms was the hardest thing I had ever done. I watched how the paramedics treated him with dignity, and honoring our love, allowed me to ride with them to the morgue. I was given his final remains after the cremation, including the thin, gold wedding band I had placed on his finger to symbolize my love for him. After all was said and done, I distributed the ashes as he had instructed, but kept a makeshift memorial in our bedroom where we promised to grow old together. Each morning, I greeted him as if he were still there. I kept the ashes on a small table next to the recliner, with his wedding band in a box.

I fielded the telephone calls, only wanting to speak to his mother and mine. Mark's mom and I shared laughs and stories of him, needing to remember him as he was. I made a promise to her that I would visit soon and ended the conversation by saying, "I love you."

My mother offered her shoulder to share my pain and loss. Again, before ending the conversation, I made the same promise of visiting soon, but I needed today to be alone.

I took the day off from work to just sit with my thoughts of Mark. Everywhere I turned or looked, he was there. I missed him so much. As day made way for night, I decided to remember him by going to Henry's for dinner. I was lucky enough to grab the table where we sat on our first date. I remembered the anxiety of meeting him that night, but smiled at the thought. The door continued to swing open with customers coming and going. I ordered a basket of onions rings, hoping that he would miraculously appear. But each time, I was disappointed. There were folks heading to the jukebox to drop quarters for their favorite selections. As I signaled for the waiter to grab the check, Mark gave me a sign. I heard it coming from the jukebox:

"... for every moment that I've spent hurting
There was a moment that I spent, ah just loving you."

He was still with me.

As I was going through the house after Mark's death, I came across a manila folder with instructions to open, only after a year had passed since Mark's death. Each time I thought of him, I found myself wanting to break the seal of the envelope that was addressed to me, but I didn't want to betray him like that. I also felt it wouldn't help the situation. I was still in a constant state of mourning over losing him. Much like Henry's, I found myself strolling the blocks of the flea market on the Hill, reminiscing of the moments Mark and I had spent hours on the weekends, walking through and seeking out hidden treasures. Our friends kept their eyes on me to make sure I didn't lose it, or lose the memory of Mark in my life. Sometimes they would stop by, and we would spend the evenings sharing stories of Mark and how much better the world was having him here. It sometimes saddened me to have those emotions brought up, but it was also great to know that his life and his love had touched so many others in this world.

I took the envelope with me to Mr. Henry's and removed it from my coat pocket. I placed it on the table, fearful of what the package contained. I looked at it as I took a sip of the drink I had asked the waiter for, to give me the courage to open it.

Without disturbing the contents, I gently opened it and removed the contents. There, before me, were photographs of my time and life with Mark. Each picture took me back to a moment where we shared life together. The crazy smiles and looks, posing for the camera, reminded me of his sense of humor. I thought how wonderful it was to have such humor in the face of what he was dealing with, what we were dealing with. I saw the candid shots that were taken, unbeknownst to us, by friends and family, who photographed moments of love shared between the two of us. It was if they were intruding on something so private between the two of us. But, I was most grateful that they were able to capture these moments for me.

Along with the photographs of our life together, were little trinkets that we shared with one another. There was a pressed rose petal from the very first rose I had given Mark for our very first Valentine's Day. Further searching revealed the ticket stubs from movies we enjoyed and the Broadway show we had taken our mothers to see. It was hard to swallow that so much of our life spent together was summed up in the few possessions now on the table in front of me. I tried to fight back the tears and wanted to kick myself for opening this can of worms so soon. I should have waited a little longer, but there was no going back.

I held up the envelope to see if anything remained, and at the moment, a letter fell out. I watched it hit the table and hesitated before I reached for it. I took a longer sip of the drink before I unfolded it and began to read:

My Dearest Kevin,

I know what you are thinking right at this moment. I can read you like a book, baby. If you are half as predictable as I think you are, and you are delving into your sentimental side, you are at Mr. Henry's right now. You are sitting in the spot where we had our very first date. You are probably working on your second basket of onion rings, watching the door closely, and thinking that maybe, just maybe, I will show up. Don't worry, I am here with you.

I smiled at the thought that he knew me so well. I noticed the tear stains from the letter and tried to remember or imagine when he had written it. I continued:

Baby, I don't want you to be sad today and I am pretty sure that you are. I know it doesn't help that I brought back a lot of old memories for you with the gifts I have left you, but you see they were wonderful moments of my life with you. I remember the one long-stemmed rose you gave me our first Valentine's Day together. Although it wilted, I was able to save one petal and press it to save for you. The pictures are moments in our life that captured the joy and love we shared with each other, and for that, I am so wonderfully blessed.

I know you were scared. I saw it on your face and at times, I felt it in your actions, but Kevin, you loved me unlike anyone else. You learned what you needed to know to be with me, you sacrificed friends to be with me, and I am truly grateful for that.

At this moment, baby, I am missing you, as I am sure you are missing me. I am loving you, as I am sure you are loving me. Of all the moments in my life, I will always remember our wedding, our union. I treasured the words you spoke from your heart that day, and I never stopped carrying them with me. Oh, what I would give to be sitting here with you tonight, sharing a smile, a drink with you, but I can't. It's not because I don't want to; it's just our circumstances. But my love, know that I am here with you in spirit. Wherever you go, I will be there; whatever you do, I will share it with you. For you are my heart.

Don't cry for me tonight, baby. Smile for me. Smile for what you gave to me and what I gave in return. Laugh with me, as we remember the true joy of love and what it feels and felt like. Love me as you did the first night we made love. Never forget what we had, because I won't. If and when you should love again, just carry a small part of me with you, because I carry you with me.

I love you, Kevin, and please don't ever forget it. You were my light in total darkness; you were the blanket that kept me warm; you were my soldier who protected me; you were my nourishment when I needed to be fed. You will always be the love of my life, and I thank you for letting me love you, I thank you for loving me, and taking care of me. I love you.

With eternal love,

Mark

I couldn't fight back the tears any longer. It seemed my tears mixed with Mark's and left smudges along the words I read. I reached for the small bottle of his ashes I had taken to wearing around my neck, to keep him with me, and looked up to the sky to see him. "I love you, too, baby."

ABOUT THE AUTHOR

Rodney Lofton was born in Seaboard, North Carolina and raised in Richmond, Virginia. His life's journey has been detailed in his first novel, a memoir entitled, *The Day I Stopped Being Pretty*.

Lofton had a dream at an early age of becoming an actor. He remembers vividly the days of sitting in the movie theaters of downtown Richmond, to view the great actors and actresses on screen. From that moment, he began to lose himself in the great lives of the characters portrayed.

At the age of ten, he auditioned for the television show, *Palmerstown, USA*. Although he lost out on the role, the acting bug had bitten. Throughout his high school years, he auditioned and landed roles in his high school productions of *The Wizard of Oz, Don't Bother Me I Can't Cope*, and a class project "Oh Freedom," in which he played the tragic mulatto son of a slave and slave master. During this time, he discovered he was different from the other guys in the neighborhood. He realized he was gay.

His journey took him to New York City, where his childhood dream came true. He began working as a publicist for a public relations firm, where he represented the likes of Kool and the Gang, Mary Wilson of the legendary girl group The Supremes and a host of others. He continued to make a name for himself, as a freelance writer for the national teen publication, *SPICE*

Magazine, providing reviews and feature articles on the top R&B/Hip-Hop performers in the music industry. His voice also provided a "biting" commentary of gossip in the music trade publication, *Music Biz*.

While fulfilling this dream of being in the entertainment industry, Lofton was dealt a tragic blow that could have easily ended his career aspirations. He was diagnosed with HIV.

He retreated to the safe haven of home—Richmond, Virginia—to regroup and redefine himself. For two years, Lofton continued to freelance as he prepared for what he assumed was the end. A chance meeting with the editor of *The Malebox*, an African-American gay publication, allowed him to broaden his readership to include an African-American gay following. His articles addressed topics in Black Gay culture on dating issues, HIV/AIDS and his most popular feature, insight into the mind of a male escort.

He decided during this time to focus his energies on writing his one great work of art, a play entitled, *The Last Supper*, which premiered as a workshop at the University of Kentucky. The play addressed, indirectly, Lofton's fears associated with living with HIV and the hope of reconciling with his father.

When he beat the odds, he decided to redirect his energy by working in the HIV/AIDS community. His voice has been heard by countless young people around the country and even internationally. He has served as Keynote Speaker and Facilitator for the New Jersey World AIDS Day Celebration, the Ryan White National Youth Conference, The United States Conference on AIDS and countless others. His commitment to youth HIV prevention led him to work in the Saratov-Oblast region of Russia, assisting agencies with high rates of HIV infection among young people.

In the summer of 2005, Lofton decided to step away from HIV/AIDS work to focus on himself and his healing. Out of this period of reflection, came his "baby,"—*The Day I Stopped Being Pretty: A Memoir*—his true and gritty retelling of where he has been, how he got there and the end result of his actions. (It was nominated for a Lambda Literary Award.) He recently served as a columnist for the online GBMNews. His column focused on issues around HIV/AIDS and African-American gay men. He currently resides in Virginia.

To learn more about Rodney Lofton, please visit his website at www.rodneylofton.com or www.myspace.com/rodlofton.

TO LEARN MORE ABOUT HIV/AIDS AND WHAT YOU CAN DO TO HELP, PLEASE VISIT THE FOLLOWING:

❏ The National Minority AIDS Council
   www.nmac.org

❏ The Centers for Disease Control and Prevention
   www.cdc.gov

❏ The National Association of People with AIDS
   www.napwa.org

Or check your local health departments/districts.